THE
COLLECTOR

THE
COLLECTOR

KELLY LYNN COLBY

Cursed Dragon Ship
PUBLISHING

Copyright © 2021 by Kelly Lynn Colby

Cursed Dragon Ship Publishing, LLC

4606 FM 1960 Rd W, Suite 400, Houston, TX 77069

captwyvern@curseddragonship.com

Cover © 2020 by Stefanie Saw

Developmental Edit by Ashley Hartsell

Copy Edit by Kailey Urbaniak

ISBN 978-1-951445-16-4

ISBN 978-1-951445-15-7 (ebook)

This books is a work of fiction fresh from the author's imagination. Any resemblance to actual persons or places is mere coincidence.

To all of those who think they're alone, you're not. You just haven't found your people yet.

Chapter One

I'd rather visit my OB/GYN than step into one more secondhand store. A minefield offered just as many lovely surprises as a shop built into a historic home. If I was really lucky, there'd be a bit of residual alcohol in my system from last night's overindulgence to keep things numb.

Even though Gina and Amelia called it "antique shopping," I hadn't seen anything I'd put that label on yet. The repurposed, turn of the century buildings peddled little more than trinkets and handmade jewelry. The attempt at pulling off a quaint town center, circa *Little House on the Prairie*, fell apart after crossing the heavily trafficked road.

Since most of these stores carried innocuous junk—not old possessions—I hadn't come across any bombs yet. Still, I hadn't touched anything all day. Just in case. All kinds of baggage could be left behind on a true family keepsake, on something of value to the person who held it. A shiver coursed through my veins as unpleasant memories that weren't even mine threatened to darken the sunny day. I tucked my gloved hands deeper into my crossed arms.

I'd be fine as long as I didn't touch anything. It was bad enough to get hints of strangers' emotions; I had to avoid the complete immersion into some long-dead person's memory. They weren't suffering anymore. Why should I?

Gina waved at me from the porch of another shop. Even back in a ponytail, her shiny dark hair framed her oval face that she somehow managed to keep smooth and as bright as bleached beach sand even though she ran miles every day in the unforgiving Houston sun. Her deep brown eyes reflected her mother's Vietnamese heritage in both shape and kindness while her exuberance and pension for using "y'all" came from her European-descendant father from east Texas. "Fauna, Amelia, come on. This one's my favorite."

Her hair bounced as she stepped over the threshold. She obviously didn't drink the bottle and a half of wine I did last night.

Amelia propped a foot on the bottom step to re-tie her shoe. "I do love shopping, but I can't seem to match Gina's energy level."

"Maybe we should start running marathons with her."

Amelia scoffed. Her short-cropped ginger head had darkened over the years, but the color still emphasized her freckles. After freshman year, she'd learned make-up tricks to hide what she had considered flaws in her skin. Recently, she'd taken on a "love me as I am or go fuck yourself" attitude. I kind of loved the change. "Never. My lounging time is sacred."

The tiny bell on the door jangled as Gina shook it back and forth, encouraging us to hurry.

I hopped around Amelia. "I'm coming."

I wished I could be myself and disregard what others felt about me. It was a whole different matter when you could *actually* feel what they thought about you. Not for the first time, I was grateful that I couldn't read minds. Experiencing others' emotions was confusing enough.

The old home's fresh paint brightened the siding. A carved wooden sign reading "Finishing Touches" swung from the door. The stair railing solidly held my weight without the squish of rotten wood. At least the owner maintained this place. A quick glance in the window showed eclectic, but obviously new, Halloween decorations next to stylized jack-o-lanterns. They seemed to be imitating a craft store's holiday display, only with a funkier selection and less hot glue.

This store should be relatively safe. Maybe I'd find something unique to display at Chipped. My computer slash cellphone repair store could use some seasonal flair. I mean, I'd never decorated before, but there could be a first. Maybe Gina's enthusiasm was rubbing off on me. A little.

I caught the door as Gina released it. The smell of mildew and retirement savings hit me in the face. A light squirmy feeling rolled my stomach. Maybe I shouldn't have eaten those nachos with the questionable cheese.

Gina rocked back and forth from heel to toe, then pointed at my hands. "I don't know how you stand those things when it's ninety degrees outside."

Amelia closed the door and pushed her sunglasses to sit on her head like an extra set of eyes. "Says the girl wasting air conditioning by leaving the door open."

I displayed the soft brown leather like a surgeon with freshly scrubbed hands. "Better safe than sorry."

My friends thought I was some sort of germaphobe since I never went without my layer of protective wear. Bacteria had no emotions; at least, none that I could feel. I had no fear of them whatsoever, but I let everyone believe as they wished. The truth was so much harder to explain. Since I'd never met anyone else like me, I'd decided long ago it was better to be seen as neurotic than full-on crazy.

To assure my friends I was fine, I changed the subject. "Isn't this where you bought those cute snowmen last year?"

Gina squeaked in excitement. "Yes! The little ceramic snowmen dressed up like the three bears with Goldilocks trying on their noses. I couldn't get enough of it. Dorian, the owner, gave me the artist's name and he just sent a newsletter announcing his new shipment. I must add to my collection." Her fingers fluttered together as if she were a classic villain plotting to take over the world.

As I followed excited Gina and protective Amelia to the register, a tingle touched the back of my neck. Our years of friendship allowed me such familiarity with their typical feelings that they floated on the surface behind my consciousness like a security blanket. What I felt now was wholly different. Maybe this place wasn't as innocuous as I imagined. Whatever this person experienced had to be so overwhelming that it leaked from their pores and filled the air like rolling fog.

I closed my eyes and rubbed my arms, trying to calm my nerves. *The feelings aren't mine.* My lungs tightened, and red spots impaired my vision. With every step, the assault intensified. Why couldn't people keep control of their emotions instead of sending them into the universe to torture me?

I was no martyr. Feeling this stressed person's emotions wouldn't relieve them of the pain anyway; so, I focused on escape. Right now.

I turned toward the exit.

"Wait, Fauna." Amelia peeked around the corner. Her flip flops smacked her feet in an eager rhythm. "You've got to see this old furniture. Apparently, it belonged to the original owner of this historic home. They use them to display the art now."

I flinched as she touched my shoulder, a reflex I'd tried to overcome through the years. Yet, the overemotional person hovering in the store somewhere had me on edge. I took a breath and allowed Amelia's familiarity to quell the panic. I could do this. People came into Chipped all the time completely distraught about losing a term paper or getting locked out of their laptop. As long as I didn't touch them, I was fine. I could handle whatever waited around the corner as well.

As Amelia guided me, a turbulent wall of unbound emotion stopped me cold. No way this could be from one person. It felt like an entire family reunion of strong emotions trying to take over my psyche.

Amelia's eyebrows knit. "What's wrong?"

"I..." I heard murmurings in my head like I'd touched an impression, a really strong one that was passed from person to person until the conglomerate of emotions exploded from its surface into its surroundings. What kind of store was this? "I don't feel so good."

"Sit." Amelia tossed off a "do not sit on the furniture" sign and guided me toward the seat.

I tried to fight her, but fighting off the swirling emotions in the air was all I had the energy for. I fell into the cushion, sending a cloud of dust into the air. Amelia coughed, but it didn't bother me. I was hardly breathing as it was.

My hands covered my head as I tried to block the onslaught of energy. My mood swung uncontrollably from elation to devastation to sorrow. I'd never felt anything so intense. I received no images or specifics, just voices and emotions. Nothing like this had happened to me since I was young and my curse first manifested.

I had to get it under control before I passed out. I focused on my own grounding memory of my mother singing her favorite hymns. Her angelic voice filled my mind like a safe barrier that drove back the attack. As the memory of Mom's voice filled the space in my head, the onslaught of rogue emotions faded to a slight humming in the back of my head.

Amelia squatted in front of me until my eyes met hers. One deep breath later, I nodded that I was okay.

"Excuse me, ma'am. You can't sit on that. It's an antique." An older woman crossed her arms and stared down at us over the frames of her reading glasses stuck on the end of her nose. Her white, permed hair and big, red apron tied around a round body reminded me of Mrs. Claus. Her stern expression reminded me of my college librarian.

Amelia sprang to her feet, standing between me and Mrs. Claus.

From around the corner, Gina sized up the situation with one look. It wouldn't be the first time these two amazing friends had saved me. They think it's migraines. If only that were the problem.

Gina tapped the disapproving older woman on the shoulder. "Dorian, I'm really interested in these pumpkins reenacting little red riding hood. Do you have a box for them?" She held up the ceramic piece.

Dorian's face lightened as she turned to her potential customer. "Of course, my dear. I'll go fetch it for you." She gestured to a display around the corner, but kept her feet firmly planted. "Did you see the scarecrows in a Rapunzel pose? The details of the straw hair are brilliant."

I leaned forward and pushed myself up from the sunken chair. That seemed to satisfy Dorian. She pivoted on her Sketchers and headed to the back. Gina winked at me as she followed.

I would have winked back, but the voices were so distracting —a deep baritone, a screaming child, a pathetic moaning.

I had to get out of there. Rushed and disoriented, I wasn't sure which way was which and I must have headed deeper into the store.

Amelia stepped around a display case to keep up with my pace. "Fauna? Are you sure you're okay? We could leave."

As much as I wanted to explain what was happening to me, where would I even start? Normal people didn't sense others' emotions. They certainly didn't experience memories left behind on objects. And I wasn't talking about loving events, like birthday parties or family dinners. No. For a memory to stick around, it had to be strong, like on the life-changing level. Those kinds of remnants were rarely pleasant.

My skin tingled with the tiny pressure of hundreds of crawling ants. I resisted the urge to itch. I'd never experienced anything so dramatic without having touched the source. My muscles didn't twitch. My gut didn't roil. Wherever these originated, it wasn't from a living source.

A strong voice rose above the noise. *Don't fight it. Embrace your gift and come find me.*

I turned in a circle trying to see all around me at once. "Who was that?" Why was someone shouting in aa mostly empty store?

Amelia shrugged. "Just Dorian, the owner. Apparently, she's a bit protective of her inventory."

I shook my head. "No, I mean the man's voice."

Amelia's forehead wrinkled, and her head cocked in a perfect reflection of my own confusion. She hadn't heard anything.

What I heard wasn't a customer.

Don't fight it. Embrace your gift and come find me. The message repeated, more like a recording than a trapped memory.

My fear subsided as curiosity took over. *Where is that coming from?*

Gina's delighted giggle ahead warned me of Dorian's presence. "These are adorable!"

I didn't want to run into the stuffy owner. Turning the other direction, with Amelia at my heels, I pushed past an awkwardly placed faux fireplace to a wall of overstuffed curio cabinets. In the corner, between displays crammed with inventory, stood the torso of a wooden man on a thigh-high pedestal, his piecemeal face level with my own. The impressions radiated from him, warping the surrounding air like heat waves. That had to be why my skin itched.

I'd had this ability as far back as I could remember. But this —I had never felt anything like it. And I had certainly never seen waves of memories vibrating around an object.

I swallowed my fear as I drew near the statue. Like one of those old Hitchcock movies, the rest of the room turned into a tunnel and the statue moved toward me. What could this thing be that was so powerful it attracted my attention all the way from the door?

Various elements of wood and metal had been melded into one cohesive piece, the upper body of a man. It reminded me of an automaton I'd seen at a fair once. Instead of an emotionless machine, it exuded intense remnants left behind by people.

Who could put together such a piece? And why? One gloved hand rubbed my nose as I contemplated the possibilities.

Maybe there was someone else like me, another cursed person. How else could they gather so many items impressed with memories? I had never met anyone like me. I had been certain I was the only one.

Hope weakened my fear. Maybe I wasn't alone in this isolating quirk. I had to find the artist. I had to know this impossible collection wasn't just a coincidence.

Chapter Two

The voice repeated the invitation. *Don't fight it. Embrace your gift and come find me.*

It definitely emanated from the automaton.

Or this was the latest manifestation of my insanity. The hymn on repeat in my head grew as annoying as the disembodied voices. Yet, I didn't know what would happen if I relinquished my only tool to control the onslaught. I had to figure out what was going before I truly lost it.

There had to be a clue on the statue itself. If I touched it with my bare skin, my mind would plummet into the scene with me starring in the first-person role. Hopefully, understanding would bleed through without having to torture myself. My gloved hand hovered a breath away from an arm that looked like half a child's baseball bat. A blur of a swing followed by triumphant joy prickled in the back of my mind. This remnant was too old to be the source of the voice on repeat, because that deep baritone sounded fresh and, somehow, modern.

It had to be coming from somewhere. The guts of a music box stood in for the vocal cords. I guess that would make logical sense. I got as close as I could without touching the pieces surrounding it.

Four or five images swirled in my head, followed by a bout of dizziness. I puffed out a breath of air with my eyes closed. Too many impressions fought for attention. I'd have to touch a piece to drive the rest away. I hated this part, but couldn't think of a way to avoid it and still get answers. How badly did I want to find someone else like me?

As I hesitated, my eye twitched, pulling my focus behind me.

Too close to block completely, Amelia's worry added to the chaos. "Are you okay?"

I had to get her to back off. Her fresh and vibrant stress rippled through the summoning voice. As much as I appreciated her concern for me, I needed space before I completely lost it.

"Just a little dehydrated. Do you think Gina has a water bottle?" She always carried a Mary Poppins bag that seemed to magically hold whatever we needed. Hopefully, searching Gina out would distract Amelia long enough for me to interpret the message in the statue.

"Probably. I'll go check." Amelia's bobbed hair fluffed in waves as she quickly turned back to me. "Are you sure you'll be all right?"

"Yeah, I just need some water." I smiled in what I hoped wasn't a grimace, as I fought the tears threatening to pour down my face from the throbbing pain in my head.

Her forehead crinkled, but she left to find Gina anyway. Her determined gait disturbed the emotional waves from the statue. I couldn't get over the fact that I could *see* the impressions. The energy produced by them emanated in the air. Despite my constant paranoia about encountering one unprepared, impressions were rare. This conglomeration of memories from different times and places had to mean I wasn't alone. Who else could collect all of these pieces into one statue? The artist had to be cursed like me.

My fingers closed into fists as I realized what I had to do. When I touched a remnant, I experienced everything the person did during the dramatic event that caused the impression to latch on to the item. It was like the most realistic—and sadistic —virtual reality imaginable. I'd never done it on purpose.

At this point, my need to not be the only one outweighed my fear at what I would experience when someone else's memory flooded my soul. Either I take a chance or remain alone forever.

Though my hands shook, I slipped a leather glove off. Before I changed my mind, I thrust a single finger at the music box.

As soon as my skin made contact, my body seemed to plunge into cold water as every pore shook with grief. My baby girl was gone. I'd never see her again. I rocked on the pink carpet she loved so much, as "Send in the Clowns" tinned from the slowly turning ballerina.

I yanked my finger off and rubbed my chest to loosen the weight that pressed against it. I didn't have a daughter. This wasn't my grief. I flung a tear from my cheek in frustration at my inability to separate myself from these remnants of another's life. The reality of what the cursed artist had to endure to assemble this statue—this beacon to one such as himself— impressed me. If I could find him, maybe he could teach me how to control it.

I wiped my sweaty hand on my jeans as I decided on a new target. The nose of the wooden man, embedded in the center of the ball-shaped head, looked like the handle of something. Maybe an artist's tool? That could be the clue.

As soon as the tip of my finger touched, agony tore through my gut. The face of my murderer was shadowed by the light of the dining room chandelier. I coughed, unable to breathe as he yanked the knife out of me. My own steaming blood dripped on my face before he plunged the blade into my chest again. I grabbed at the weapon. He leaned close to me as his bright blue eyes danced with glee. Then his lips curled as he pushed the blade all the way through to the floor. I screamed, but nothing came out. I couldn't breathe. I couldn't...

My shoulders vibrated as my head rocked side to side on a

squeaky wooden floor. A shadow leaned over me, shaking me. I threw my arms up to deflect another blow.

Amelia's voice broke through the vision. "Fauna? Fauna, speak to me. You are *not* alright." She turned her head to Gina on my other side. "Call 911."

I waved her off with my tingling arm. "I'm fine. I'm fine. I don't need an ambulance." The agonizing pain and rush of adrenaline faded leaving me shivering and achy.

I had to find this artist, this person who had the same curse. And when I did, I was going to punch him in the nose for tormenting me. Why not an ad in the newspaper, jerk?

Sucking in air delicately, grateful to be able to breathe again, I pushed up from the floor to prove I could. My numb lower body threatened my balance. I was sure I'd end up back on the ground.

Dorian sidled over and placed a wood stool behind me. "Are you sure you're okay?"

"Yes. I'm good." I hoped my voice didn't give away the terror that still lurked in my mind. I tried to sound casual. "I do love that piece there though. I wonder if I could have the name of the artist?"

The air still vibrated around the automaton, but I couldn't hear anything from it. My mother's voice filled in all the space in my mind, and I hadn't even consciously cued up the hymn.

Dorian crossed her arms; her forehead grew extra wrinkles. I didn't have to sense her emotions to know she was annoyed. "That's Albert Johnson's work. He disappeared from the art scene about a year ago."

Gina leaned close to the statue's face. "It's amazing, all the pieces put together to make this tin man looking thing."

I put my glove back on and bit my tongue to resist the urge to scream at her not to touch it. But it wouldn't matter. The impressions couldn't hurt her. Just me.

I turned to Dorian. "Do you happen to have his contact

information? I'd love to get a custom piece." I was proud of myself for sounding almost completely normal.

The store owner dropped her hands and cocked her hip. "I'm sure I can dig up what I have when I write up the bill of sale."

That's great. She wanted to take my money along with my dignity. I sighed deeply as exhaustion set in. "I'll take it."

Amelia shook her head at me and pointed at a tiny yellow sticker stuck to the pedestal. "Are you sure, Fauna?"

I wasn't going to get close again. I couldn't risk touching it and passing out from another strong impression. I'd save *that* embarrassment for my own kitchen floor. "I'm sure."

"Wonderful. It's a unique piece that will immediately draw in your guests." Dorian clapped her hands like a gavel proclaiming the final verdict.

Guests? Not likely. Besides, what would the entertainment value be? Watch our hostess pass out in front of this inert statue for no apparent reason?

I followed Dorian to the register and pulled out my emergency credit card. This qualified as an emergency. I was not the only one cursed. Someone else had been dealing with this and was comfortable enough to call out more like him. Nothing could possibly be more important than that.

"That'll be $3000 even." Dorian pointed to the scanner.

As I swallowed heavily and I inserted the plastic, my fingertips tingled from Dorian's joy. At least someone was having a good day.

Chapter Three

U sually my sanctuary, my townhouse vibrated with the energy of the tightly wrapped statue. Gina adjusted the base in the corner between the modest kitchen and the glass dining room table.

Amelia tucked a blanket around my knees and handed me a glass of water. "If you need anything, throw up the bat signal and I'll be here."

This was why I couldn't confess what was really wrong. Mama Amelia would freak out and take me in for testing. "I'm just dehydrated, I'm sure."

Gina half-dragged Amelia from my condo. "Well, make sure to drink tons of water before we go out Wednesday. No messing up my last few girls' nights on weeknights right before school starts. It's too hard dealing with second graders *and* a hangover."

"You got it." I lifted the water bottle in my lap to prove I understood. As annoying as their attention was right now, I don't know how I'd survive without my girls.

But this I had to do alone. After the deadbolt clicked on the door, I threw the blanket off.

Like at the store, waves floated around the statue, though the packaging dulled the effect. Still, there was no way that thing could stay here with me. The voices would keep me up all night. I still couldn't scrub the memory of the murdered woman, her warm blood dripping down her cheeks, the sound of her ribs cracking. I prayed they caught the guy.

From my purse, I took out the receipt with the information that was supposed to answer all of my questions. Dorian's loopy handwriting spelled out a PO Box in Austin. Useless. What was I supposed to do with this? Track down the location and wait for someone wearing gloves in the middle of summer to check his mail?

I sat at my dining room table and reached for my laptop. Electronics were a safe touch item. For some reason, they didn't hold a remnant memory. At least, I hadn't found a single instance of an experience captured on one. It was the reason I was drawn to computers to begin with both in college and as a career with Chipped.

Maybe Google held the answers to this mysterious artist. I removed my gloves to better control my mousepad. The first search turned up way too many Albert Johnson's. By adding "artist," a small show in Austin over a year ago popped up.

"Up and coming mixed media artist, Albert Johnson, came all the way from Houston to be featured at Roseworks Gallery for the month of June."

"Mixed Media?" That was putting it lightly. I scrolled down to the only picture in the article. Next to the overpriced monstrosity currently lurking in the corner of my dining room stood a stunning black man, his body cocked at a confident angle.

I don't know what I expected. That artists were so eccentric they didn't fit into normal categories of attractiveness? I mean, they were supposed to suffer for their art, right?

Well, Albert Johnson didn't *look* like he was suffering. He was gorgeous. Maybe twenty-five years old, his muscles pushed against his tight polo and form-fitting jeans. His hand rested on the head of the automaton. The caption read, "Johnson sourced the pieces for Walter, featured in the photo, from all over Austin."

How curious that it came back to Houston. Maybe it didn't sell? The article didn't offer any further answers. Something bothered me though. What was I missing?

My discarded gloves shifted in my lap as I lifted the bottle of water.

"Gloves!" He wasn't wearing any. And his hand rested comfortably on the statue that knocked me on my ass.

My heart sank in disappointment. He couldn't be cursed like me.

I slammed the laptop closed and stalked to the kitchen. It was time for something stronger than water.

Walter, as his creator apparently called him, mocked me in the corner as I popped the cork on a bottle of wine.

Now I was stuck with this thing that would torment me every moment I was home, the only place where I could relax. Maybe I should have had Amelia and Gina leave it on the lawn for the garbage man. That would have been fun to explain. I'm so pathetically lonely that I spent two months' mortgage on a nightmare just for the minuscule chance that I could find someone, just one more person, who understood. But did he?

If Albert wasn't cursed, how did he manage to find all of these remnants? And why did one piece of the statue call out to be found? If the artist wasn't the one, he had to know who was.

The alcohol warmed my skin. No more thinking. It was time to act.

I grabbed scissors out of the junk drawer in the kitchen and marched to the statue. My mother's voice singing "Be Still My Soul" repeated in my mind to block the incoming flood of impressions. Before fear froze my actions, I cut through the thick tape and ripped the brown paper.

The wave of emotions beat over me like an icy tide.

"Alright, Albert Johnson or whoever's voice I'm hearing, tell me how to find you."

Seeming to answer me, Walter chanted, *Don't fight it. Embrace your gift and come find me.*

I focused on his voice, driving every competing impression back into its corresponding object. The message tingled through me as I gave it control. My hands flared like they were holding a ball. My skin crawled as I allowed the impression to influence me when my usual MO called for me to block them at all costs. The ball in my hand—well, in the hand of the speaker at the time he left the impression—had contours and weighed less than I would have guessed based on its size. My gaze fell to it. More accurately, the man's gaze stared at the globe in his hands, and I came along for the ride. A globe, like one of those you'd find in an old classroom, but dull and sepia-colored instead of the modern blues and greens.

I blinked to bring the statue back into focus. Where would a globe be? That was when I noticed the continents carved into Walter's round head.

That was where Albert touched the statue in the newspaper article. Was that a hint or a coincidence?

Welp. I either go to bed or do this thing. The last swallow of wine slipped down my throat. I cracked my knuckles and placed my fingertips only on the sphere.

As soon as I made contact, all tension left my body.

Albert, or whoever left the message, was calm. More than calm, comforting. I'd never felt such an impression before. I'd always believed that peaceful feelings lacked the intense energy needed for a remnant memory. Somehow, the cursed voice had managed to create an impression on purpose. Imagine how much more he could teach me.

I closed my eyes to focus on the message playing in my head. In the memory, a street sign swayed beside a traffic light: Bagby. I knew that part of Houston well. I would have bought a condo there if I could've afforded it.

Acid sloshed in my stomach as the image jumped ahead to an apartment building. No, that wasn't quite right. They were condos with wrought iron balconies and Hardiplank siding that began light blue close to the street and darkened to deep navy at the top floor. I thought I recognized that building across the street from my favorite Mexican restaurant.

The image jumped again. My stomach couldn't tolerate much more. A bright red door with curly numbers affixed above the peek hole declared the condo 413.

What was with the melodrama? Couldn't he have just written the address on the damn thing? Of course, anyone could have found him then. I can't imagine going through all this trouble to find someone like you, another cursed person, only to have a stalker show up.

Then the familiar words repeated as the door opened, *Don't fight it. Embrace your gift and come find me.*

The vision popped back to the beginning and the Bagby street sign. I blinked my eyes open as I released Walter.

Midtown. It was only a twenty-minute drive, but it was Sunday at dinner time.

I shook my head as I bent to the floor and retrieved my gloves. I couldn't believe I was actually contemplating driving down there to confront a stranger. What if he wasn't cursed like me? Would he have a supplier who brought him these items? Maybe I should do more research before I headed out.

I'd been the only cursed person my entire life. The rest of the wine helped quell my fears. If there was the possibility of another out there, I had to know. Tonight.

Chapter Four

What do I say? I hovered in front of the elevator for ten minutes and stared at the red door at the other end of the hallway. My heart raced as if I'd just finished a marathon.

Nope. I can't do this. I pressed the elevator button. What was I thinking driving out here to bang on the door of a complete stranger and demand answers for questions I didn't know how to ask? The elevator doors slid open and I took one step.

My muscles tensed, refusing to move any further.

If Albert really was cursed and he could so effortlessly co-exist with the remnants that tortured me, maybe he could teach me the trick, show me how to control this curse. If I walked away now, I could be alone forever, stuck in this not-life.

The only real connections to humanity I had were Gina and Amelia. What would happen if they married and had families and left me behind? I never dared dream of a husband and children and PTA meetings and strolls on the beach. But maybe I could have that with Albert's help. Maybe he could teach me how to be normal.

I had to take the chance. In one determined movement, I pivoted on my heels, marched down the hall, and knocked on number 413. On its own, the door swung open before I had a chance to drop my fist.

Doubt flooded my mind as the smell of rotten food wafted from the darkness. My forearm blocked my nose. Over the foul odor, flowed more emotional remnants. I hadn't considered the possibility there would be other pieces at his place. I should have finished that bottle of wine before I headed over here. A little numbing would be a welcome gift. My gloves hugged my hands as I steeled my resolve.

A metal rack stacked tightly with eclectic pieces practically vibrated with impressions. I marveled at the cultivated collection. Albert, or his partner, must have combed the state to amass these objects imbedded with memories. I had come across only a few in my entire lifetime. Was he putting together statues and placing them all over the city? Like a kind of calling card for cursed people to track him down? How many of us could there possibly be?

What was I getting myself into?

"Albert!" My voice echoed against the dark walls, like these shelves were the only furniture in the place. "I should probably just leave, but you summoned me. Albert, err—" my mother's hymn in my mind turned to her voice admonishing me for my lack of manners, "Mr. Johnson, are you here?"

A dim light beckoned me further into the apartment. That smell turned my stomach. He couldn't be here. No one would leave food to rot that long without tossing it. What was next? I guess I could leave him a note.

It felt strange to leave my details after breaking into a stranger's home, but I wasn't sure what else to do. Around the shelves I was careful not to touch, a small Victorian stained-glass lamp offered a bit of light. On its table sat a notepad and a pencil roughly carved, like with a pen knife instead of a formal school sharpener.

Something was really wrong, but I couldn't figure out what it was. The impressions beating my brain made it difficult to think clearly. My hands shook as I reached for the writing utensil. "I'm leaving you a note, Mr. Johnson. If you're here, I'll... dammit." The pencil slipped from my hands and rolled toward the kitchen. It stopped abruptly in a drop of liquid.

When I retrieved it, all I could think was how gross this apartment was. As I turned the pencil in my hand, the thick fluid was almost gel-like. The pale lamp light reflected off a deep red, almost purple pigment.

What is this? Curry maybe. Or rancid ketchup. My heart beat faster as something deep down, something under the haze of the wine, told me it wasn't a condiment. Before I had time to question my actions, I used the light from my phone to follow the trail around the faux wall between the kitchen and living area.

All other emotions, mine and those of the impressions, vanished in an instant, and all I felt was shock. The light rippled as tremors shook my hands. Sprawled in the middle of the black and white classic tiles lay the mutilated corpse of Albert Johnson.

Chapter Five

I barely made it to the front door before every meal I ever ate poured out of me. After I purged enough to catch my breath, I noticed the blood-dipped pencil still clutched in my gloved hand. It fell from my grip and I rubbed the coagulated blood on the wall.

I wiped my mouth with the back of my unstained glove. This was not what I signed up for. Obviously, he couldn't answer any questions. It wasn't like I could speak to the dead. I had to get out of there.

As I fled to the elevator, my conscience tore at my resolve. I couldn't just leave him there.

Alone.

Mutilated.

I pivoted and headed back for the red door.

The acidic smell of vomit mixed with rot from the bloody corpse overwhelmed my nasal passages. What do people do in these circumstances?

Scenes from my favorite crime procedurals popped into my mind. I'd never be able to watch another with the same sort of detachment. I understood stumbling across a murder victim in a visceral way now. What was I supposed to do?

I almost snapped my fingers as I remembered. Call 911 of course.

"This is 911. Where are you calling from?" The woman's voice was so calm and logical she helped focus my panic.

I took a deep breath and spouted out the address.

"Thank you," she said. "Can you tell me what your emergency is?"

"My emergency?" What was I supposed to tell her? I followed an invitation from an artist psychically embedded in a statue, and when I got here, the artist was a dead body. It sounded totally reasonable. I was sure she would send a padded wagon instead of a paddy wagon. My hand massaged my forehead. "I found a dead guy on the floor of his condo."

"Is the victim breathing?"

"Breathing?" Oh my god, I hadn't checked. What if he was still alive and I wasted this precious time in panic?

My guilt overrode my fear as I re-entered the crime scene. The shelf of impressions hummed as I walked past, but I didn't get any details. I didn't have the energy to listen.

By the kitchen, blood splattered the floor more aggressively than I'd noticed the first time. Bile burned my esophagus at the shoe prints on the tile. Shit, I contaminated the crime scene on my flight, didn't I?

The streetlamps glowed through the kitchen window, casting the scene in a jaundiced light. Death's gray haze discolored Albert's dark eyes. The picture in the black and white photo online gave him more color than he had now.

A dizzy spell washed over me. I leaned against the refrigerator so I wouldn't pass out. My imagination saw shadows move along the far wall. A quick search revealed the light switch, which I flipped on.

In life, his skin must have been a gorgeous deep brown, not the splotchy taupe that reflected the fluorescent lighting. His short, relaxed dreads blended in beautifully with his tight beard.

His death grimace was a mockery of the confident grin from the newspaper article.

The voice on the phone made me jump. I'd forgotten I was holding it. "Ma'am, are you still there? Is he breathing?"

"Not for a while now would be my guess."

"Ma'am? Can you still hear me? Uniformed officers and an ambulance are on their way to your location. ETA two minutes."

"Thank you." It was the only thing I could think to say as I hung up the phone.

I'd never seen a dead body before. Even when my grandparents died, my mom wouldn't let me attend the wake. She knew I was a sensitive child and didn't want to scar me for life. She didn't realize that my sensitivity had nothing to do with life or death. It was being assaulted with emotions I was too young to understand. It made me close myself off from as much as I could as a sort of protective measure.

Did he do the same thing? Albert Johnson died alone. Was this my future? What if he was the only other person like me on the planet, the only hope I had to free me from this isolation?

The murderer couldn't get away with this, with taking away the only bit of hope for answers I had, with causing this beautiful man to die in agony. I dropped to my knees in the clean spot by his head. My gloves came off before I knew what I was doing.

My logical mind screamed at me. The shows said not to touch anything. Then again, I'd already screwed up with my footprints. My emotional mind, the part that held the curse, prodded me along. If I could see the murderer, I could give his description to the police. I could at least point them in the right direction. If this was me, I'd want some sort of justice.

Before reason won the battle, I put both hands on the shoulders of Albert's plaid, button-up shirt. The turmoil of a murder left a strong impression and my mind plunged into the storm.

I scrambled into the kitchen and slipped on the tile floor. The man chasing me dropped on top and banged my head on the floor, stunning me. I felt no pain, but my body vibrated with adrenaline. Yet, I couldn't seem to make my limbs fight back.

"Stop it! This isn't happening to me. Separate." Talking out loud seemed to help build a gap between real and memory.

The edges of my sight darkened as I concentrated on Albert's perspective and tried to keep it his. The attacker grabbed a knife from the counter and pricked Albert's neck as he threatened him. "Where is it?"

"You?" Fear tightened my bowels as Albert recognized his pursuer.

He was white with dark hair, but his more identifying features were covered in shadow. If only he'd been facing toward the kitchen window, then I could have seen something.

"Yes, me. You didn't think you could keep it up forever, did you?" The knife wielder growled more than talked. "Where is it?"

My chin tingled at a cut of the knife as Albert shook his head no. "That was a long time ago. I don't know where it ended up."

At that moment, I knew Albert Johnson *was* the owner of the voice from Walter. I'd found him. Joy lifted my dread until I remembered these were the last memories of a dead man. Had I missed my opportunity?

Fully straddling Albert, the attacker's face was still hidden, but I could make out scars on his forearm, like he had attempted suicide. His shoulders slumped, which cued a rush of fear from Albert, who renewed his squirming. My heart sped up with his. He must have sensed something from his attacker, but I couldn't feel that man's emotions on Albert. Had he not felt anything as he attacked another human being? Or maybe it wasn't intense enough to leave behind a remnant? Or Albert's emotions could be so strong that it drowned anything from his attacker? It wasn't like I'd done a case study. I was far from an expert on impressions. I wasn't even sure how they worked.

Albert's voice rose in pitch. "I haven't said anything to anybody. A deal's a deal."

Albert bounced his hips to knock loose the man pinning him down, but the attacker was too strong for the smaller artist.

"I've heard that before." The knife plunged into Albert's chest. "This way no one will find it."

Albert screamed, and I screamed as his agony ripped through my chest. He tried to turn away from the repeated blows, but he couldn't breathe. The teeth of the attacker reflected the dull light from the living room as he leaned into the knife hilt, forcing a gush of blood to bubble out.

Then something changed. Albert's emotions morphed from fear to agony to—joy. He laughed.

The attacker took both the dying man's cheeks in his hands. Tears poured from Albert's eyes. His mutilated chest tortured him, but surfing on top of all that pain was something else. I could feel it in my fingertips and toes. Happiness.

I'd never experienced anything like that. Did Albert want to die?

Albert giggled like he was being tickled by an outside force. A reflection of what he experienced, my diaphragm ached from the strain of mingling screams and laughs. It was difficult enough to get air in at all through the excruciating wounds.

I could feel him weakening, everything faded and became less intense. Albert's fog as he neared death allowed me to separate my experience from his. Those were not my wounds. My centering force, my mother's voice, sang in the background. I even managed to tap a finger to the beat. With my true physical form partially isolated from Albert's, I forced myself to concentrate on the murderer's face.

His features drifted in and out of focus through Albert's blurred vision. Pieces of a face, high cheek bones, a nondescript nose, a glimpse of bright blue eyes.

"Oh," the killer said, seeming to understand something I did not. "Of course."

He kissed Albert's face and stood up. "Thank you."

The joy left Albert and all he could do was struggle to

breathe. His hand scraped the floor after the man who just killed him.

"I won't make the same mistake." The murderer held Albert down with a foot as he yanked the knife from his chest.

The pain faded as Albert's eyes blinked closed. A bitter sense of disappointment for something undone coated the last layer of the impression.

I tore my grip from his shirt before he took his last breath. Tears fell from my face as my lungs worked at breathing. I didn't know if that was enough. I couldn't see the man clearly at all. Why had Albert kept his condo so dark? I thought artists liked light. If it had only been brighter, I could have helped.

My fear turned to anger at my impotence. What good was this stupid curse if I couldn't use it to help someone?

An officer froze in the doorway of the kitchen, his gun pointed at me, as he shouted, "Don't move!"

Chapter Six

C ops flooded the condo building. A few uniformed officers questioned the neighbors who gawked at the macabre scene. I leaned against a wall in the hallway rocking my shoulders, trying not to look at my vomit all over the floor or make eye contact with the loitering people and their fake grief. If any of them actually cared about Albert, they would have called someone long before I showed up. Also, the fingers pointing my way put me on edge.

No one had talked to me since the officer who first confronted me in the kitchen. I told him I'd seen someone flee the scene and wanted to give a description. Though it was all bullshit, I hoped my Oscar-worthy performance convinced him. The bags wrapped around my fingers seemed to testify to the opposite.

The homicide detectives had been in the apartment for at least a half an hour before one came out and approached me. Short, but well built, his gray suit looked tailored around his strong shoulders and thin waist. It was not what I expected from a cop's paygrade. I thought he looked of Latin descendent based on his honey skin tone paired with the subtle waves in his deep brown hair. This was Houston though. He could just as easily be a dark-skinned Greek or Italian. What threw me off were his eyes. The haunting amber color seemed to read me.

I had the urge to confess everything. So instead, I threw out my lie. "I saw a guy run from here. I think I can describe him."

The detective raised a bushy, though not obnoxiously so, eyebrow. He pulled out his phone, seemingly comfortable with long pauses that made me want to jump in with more confessions. He tapped a few things in. "That's what Officer Pradock said." He held his hand out for me. "I'm Inspector Flores and you are—"

Latino it was then. I pulled my hands from behind my back to reveal the plastic bags the crime scene people insisted on putting around them for evidence. "Fauna Young."

He rubbed his unshaven chin. "You touched things, didn't you?"

My gaze unconsciously drifted to the mess I made in the hallway. Flores followed my focus and took more notes in his phone. "What did you see?"

The memory of the shadowed face shifted across my mind. He looked like almost every white guy I'd ever seen. If only I could separate the feelings from the vision, maybe I could concentrate and get a better picture. "It was a white guy with blue eyes." I realized what an idiot I sounded like. "I'm sorry. It was dark and with only the light from the kitchen window..."

Flores took notes on his phone, but I couldn't shake the feeling that he didn't believe a word I said. Or maybe it was my own guilt at not being a better witness. I could be a lot more accurate if I was allowed to watch the impression again. I didn't know which scared me more, explaining to the detective what I could do or experiencing the murder again.

"How tall was he?"

Shit. I didn't see him standing. Even if I had, it would've been from Albert's point of view. How tall was the artist? My head throbbed with the complexity of the situation. "Um, taller than me? He had dark hair and seemed to be in pretty good shape."

My description sounded like a random jogger in Midtown. All that was missing was the designer dog. Maybe I should have just called 911 and left. I wasn't any help at all.

With a crack of his neck, Flores looked me straight in the eye. "Where were you last night?"

The question threw me. "Uh." Where was I last night? I didn't even remember what day it was. I was sure I'd stood in this hallway for eons. "That was Saturday?"

He nodded, his amber eyes bit through my skin like maybe he had the curse too.

"Out with my girlfriends." Oh crap, he thought I was a suspect. How was he going to allow me to help solve the murder if he thought I committed the crime? "You can call my girlfriends. They'll verify." Though we did go home early because the DJ sucked and Gina really wanted to go antiquing the next morning. My vision gave no confirmation of when Albert was attacked except that it was dark outside. It was selfish, I knew, but I hoped it all happened while we were still at the club. I needed my alibi to hold up.

More notes in his phone. Okay. That was enough.

"Look. I just bought a piece of Albert Johnson's work and the store owner gave me his address. I came by to—"

Flores perked up. "Albert Johnson? His neighbors called him 'The Collector' and didn't know his actual name. Apparently, it was his stage name for his artist career."

My rocking against the wall increased as adrenaline pumped through me. No wonder I couldn't find anything about the guy under his real name. He must have had a website for his art under the pseudonym. My fingernails scratched the inside of the plastic bag, itching to get to my laptop. Wait. Did knowing his real name make me look more or less like a suspect? I needed Flores to see me as an ally if I were to find answers.

After clearing my throat, I stood up straight and tried to

match Flores's confident stance, though I felt anything but. "Look. I just came to ask about his art and his door was ajar. When I saw the man lying on the floor, I called 911." I held up my fingers with blood on the tips. "The lady on the phone asked if he was still breathing. So, I checked."

Flores typed as quickly as I talked. Then waved over one of the crime scene guys. "Tyler, can you take those off and get a close look at the blood please?"

Holy shit, he might believe me. I held my breath as the lab tech approached me without questioning the detective.

Tyler had huge bags under his eyes and a slight overbite that caused him to chew on his lower lip. "Please hold still," he whispered, like making the sound was all the effort he could put forth.

I flinched as he untied the bag around each wrist and took more pictures of my hands from multiple directions. When Tyler dropped the camera around his neck and reached for my wrists with his gloved hands, I flinched reflexively. I'd had enough of other peoples' emotions for one day. Tyler blinked at me and reached for my wrist again. I blew out a steady breath and cued Mom's hymn, as his fingers touched my skin. The plastic gloves served as a measly barrier. My eyes twitched, the curse's way of expressing Tyler's stress, but it was weak. Experience had taught mee that meant exhaustion. Or everything was shorted out with the overuse today.

Flores spoke quietly with the first officer that unnecessarily pulled his gun on me. Good. He could verify that I was near Albert's head which was a perfectly reasonable spot to check for a pulse. Plus, my knees and fingers were the only part of me that had any blood on them. How could I be anything other than a witness? Maybe an idiot who should have called 911 when she noticed the smell and the open door, but only a witness, nevertheless.

After Flores finished typing into his phone, he motioned for another uniform. "Officer Turner, I need a large evidence bag and a jumpsuit."

"Yes, sir," she said.

As Flores focused on me again, I felt entirely exposed. A bit of energy surged through my veins as Tyler the tech released me.

"So?" Flores asked him.

Tyler yawned, as he explained, "I'd have to run tests to be sure, but the blood's started to break down."

Flores looked at me. "So, not fresh?"

My mouth hung open as I tried to decide if I should answer or if Tyler was supposed to.

The tech simply shook his head, while Flores kept his focus on me. Was he letting me know I was lying? Why was he letting me hear the tech's conclusion? Yes, I was lying about what I saw, but not my innocence. I should have just told him the truth. He'd have totally believed me, right?

The woman cop Flores sent off earlier returned and held up some items.

"Please find Ms. Young a private place to change, then collect her clothing." He handed the officer my driver's license. "And make sure she gets home safely."

Out of the condo door pushed the burly, older detective who had arrived with Flores. I could only assume it was his partner. "Hold up. I need to see her shoes."

Flores didn't flinch at this partner's gruff demeanor. He must be used to it. "Fauna Young, this is Detective Collins."

If Flores was tight and controlled, Collins was a whirling dervish. His mostly white hair stuck out in every direction adding no contrast or framing to his round, rosy-pale face. He gave a withering look to his partner, as if annoyed with the formalities. "Now that we are acquainted, hand over your shoes?"

Trying to balance without touching anything, I was grateful for Officer Turner's help. She removed each one with her gloved hands and dumped them in an evidence bag. I was relieved I hadn't worn my good pair of hiking boots.

Collins flipped the bag over. He shook his head as he shared his findings with Flores. "Definitely contaminated the scene."

Flores held up his hand as he looked at me from the corner of his eye.

Was he looking for a reaction? "I'm sorry. I'd never seen a dead body before." My stomach lurched as the full force of what was happening overcame my thinking mind.

Flores pulled out a business card and put it in my shaking hand. "Come by 1200 Travis tomorrow afternoon. We'll get a full statement then."

Something about the man demanded respect and I didn't have the energy to fight it. "Yes, sir."

As I followed Officer Turner to a place to change, Collins's loud whisper carried, "You're just going to let her go?"

I stopped to remove my socks to hear Flores's response.

"You know she didn't kill him, but she knows something she's not sharing. A bit of trust goes a long way."

Collins snorted. "With enough rope..."

Chapter Seven

The offices for the HPD Homicide Division looked like any other cubicle farm, except that the constant flow of people were not in khakis and polos. Rather, some were in handcuffs, some crying, some angry, and many were in uniform. The emotional deluge washed over my exhausted brain, a steady hum that made it difficult to focus. As long as I didn't touch anyone, I could keep it under control.

I hadn't slept at all last night. Maybe it would be more accurate to say early this morning. With that damn statue whispering to me, falling asleep was almost impossible. Add in the haunting visual of Albert's murder that assaulted me every time I *did* manage to close my eyes, and I counted exactly zero sheep.

When Flores walked into the precinct sipping from a steaming Styrofoam cup, something about the way he carried himself made me believe in him. Still, I rubbed my extra pair of leather gloves, trying to decide if I should take one off before shaking his hand. Then I'd know for sure if he suspected me or not. I had years of experience at reading people and translating that knowledge into useful information. Though I'd sworn never to use the curse to manipulate people again, times like this made that oath difficult to keep.

Flores nodded at me, but addressed another man behind him. "Thank you for your time, Mr. Tanner. We know where to find you if we have any follow up questions."

The tall, dark-haired gentleman in an expensive business suit shook the detective's hand. I didn't know why he was here, but holy cow was he hot from the back. Muscles stretched his jacket's shoulders as he lifted his arms to put on a pair of designer sunglasses. A ruby ring flashed in the filtered light. As he passed me headed for the glass doors, he cocked a half grin in my direction. His lip quirked up slightly higher on the left side. Happiness flowed behind him, tickling the tips of my fingers. Good thing I didn't have that glass of wine I really wanted with breakfast. I might have just followed that gorgeous specimen out the door. I could have used a little escapism after what I'd witnessed —though, admittedly, feeling happy at such a negatively charged place felt inappropriate.

Since Flores was wearing the same suit as the night before, I doubted he'd had time to make it home.

Flores held up a finger to me as another uniformed officer walked up to him with a white woman. She wore a mismatched pants suit and had her hair tied up in a messy bun. I didn't have to touch her to read her emotions. Her tear-streaked face spoke of despair and loss. Flores guided her to a hallway. I couldn't hear what he said, but his tone was soothing.

A Hispanic man with a brown fedora and pock-marked face sat on a bench with his back leaned against the wall. He wore a button-up Hawaiian shirt and cargo shorts, a contrast even in the mixed bag of the precinct. Something about him was familiar, but I couldn't place his face. His gaze dropped from the ceiling and focused directly on me. My skin crawled at the direct attention. Who was this guy?

"Rough night."

My body jumped an inch out of the seat at the unexpected voice on the other side of Flores's desk.

Detective Collins held out a bottle of water for me. "The

Collector's clients have been in one after another since the news broke of his death. Seems he'll be missed."

I swore I heard accusation in his voice. My instinct was backed up by the cramping of my gut. Collins was angry about something.

As I reached for the water, my exposed forearm brushed against something on Flores's desk. The familiar sensation of being pulled into an impression shook my core. Dammit. Not right now.

I plunged into the mind of a teenage girl. Instead of the steady flow of events like most remnants, this one cascaded one emotion over another. She must have held whatever I touched a lot. My heart beat faster at new love, then crashed to my toes with the loss. Anger at her mother was rampant in the swing of feelings. At least I could separate myself from this impression since it was so fractal.

Before I could yank my arm away, a boy's voice overtook the frantic disparity of the girl's. I'd never touched an item that held remnants from two different individuals. This was new. Curiosity encouraged me to lower my guard and let myself fully immerse in the boy's memory.

I sat on a frilly, violet bed, holding a diary with a broken lock. "She doesn't love me. Now I know the truth," I said over and over again. Everything hurt, except for my numb fingers squeezing the book. My vision blurred with tears and I didn't know how I would go on without her. I curled up on her bed for the last time, and cried, as the diary slipped from my hands.

The remnant ended abruptly. I shoved myself back from the desk. My fingers ached from numbness and I rubbed them to return feeling. That was the worst part. When I wasn't inside the impression anymore, why did my body continue to feel the aftereffects? I wasn't really there to begin with. This was one of those things that would have been nice to discuss with Albert.

I looked to see what I'd touched and the broken-lock diary the boy had held in his hand sat on top of a pile of files in an evidence bag. I remembered the water bottle Collins's had offered as it bounced off the edge of the desk and hit the ground. I crossed my arms over my chest and blinked at it as it rolled away. I couldn't seem to move myself to action.

"I got it." Flores bent down and picked it up as he headed my way.

Collins mumbled something I couldn't make out as he passed Flores, who nodded.

I still hadn't cleared my head from the impression. The teenager's words circled in my mind. The teenage boy had really loved that girl. Teenager remnants were the worst. The hormones pumped into their bodies made everything seem wonderful or horrible with very little even keeled. I would lose my mind, literally, if I was exposed to a high school environment.

With a grunt, Flores sat down heavily in his chair and placed the bottle close to me. "Did you get any sleep?"

I wanted to answer his question, but couldn't shake the impression. "She doesn't love me. Now I know the truth." As soon as I said the words, my muscles relaxed, and my mind cleared. Shit, I really needed a better way to separate myself from those experiences.

The look of confusion on Flores's face was one I'd seen before. But his reaction was unique. "What did you say?" He picked up the diary's bag and checked the seal.

Of course, it was still intact. I didn't read the damn thing. Yet, the fact that he associated my involuntary rambling to the diary showed a different way of thinking. I was right about him. He'd get to the truth and find Albert's killer.

Flores opened a desk drawer and slid the evidence bag inside. As he closed it, he studied me with those intuitive eyes. I rubbed my upper arms in discomfort. He must be good at getting confessions. That mix of concern and sternness had its own kind of power.

The arrival of a man with a pad of paper and a couple pencils interrupted the tension between us. "Detective Flores? I'm ready."

Flores stood almost too quickly and offered his seat to the new arrival. "Ms. Young, this is Horace Newman. He's the best sketch artist in the city."

"Hey, Flores, we've got another one for you," called an officer near the glass doors.

A tall Hispanic man with a pockmarked face carried a fedora in his hands beside the uniformed cop.

"I'm coming, Davis." Flores waved his acknowledgement. He paused, staring at my gloved hands, like he wanted to ask me something.

I tucked them under my knees—I wasn't about to explain—and addressed Horace. "What do you need me to do?"

Horace beat his pad of paper with the end of his pencil. "Tell me what you remember."

Concentrating was a real challenge in the emotionally messy police station. With my eyes closed, I tried to visualize what I witnessed without getting swallowed by the terror and pain. The backlight shadowed the killer's features. "He was white with blue eyes and dark hair."

I peaked at Horace who blinked at his sketchbook. I was going to have to work harder. I didn't really want to re-experience the murder, but I needed to help wherever I could. My fingers flexed in my lap as I imagined gripping Albert's shoulders. The metallic smell of blood assaulted my nose, then the eerie sound of Albert's misplaced laughter grated my nerves. It was so dark in my memory of his memory.

Then, the murderer yanked the knife and his forearms glistened in the streetlight from the window. At first, I thought he'd cut himself. Then I realized they were scars. Old ones. That had to be helpful.

"I remember his arms the clearest. Would that help?"

Chapter Eight

My fingers drummed against the steering wheel of my car while I tried to wrap my mind around walking into Chipped. It was such a normal Tuesday morning activity when nothing about the world felt normal anymore.

In less than forty-eight hours, my life shifted from being the only cursed one, to maybe finding another, to finding that person murdered, to becoming a suspect, and finally to completely failing to describe the killer. Was I now just supposed to go to work like nothing happened?

A light flipped on inside the store. Jeff must have had another fight with his wife. He never beat me in unless he'd spent the night. That somehow brought me comfort. At least some things remained the same.

Since electronic equipment never held an impression, a career in computers was a no-brainer. When working in an office full of people proved too overwhelming, I used my inheritance to open Chipped instead. Every now and then, someone— usually Amelia from her comfy desk chair in her comfy corporate position—asked for my help debugging code, but the bulk of business involved retrieving data from broken computers and fixing cracked phone screens.

Working might have been just what I needed to re-center myself. With Walter at home, it no longer qualified as a sanctuary. That damn statue had served its purpose. Maybe it was time to kick it to the curb. I didn't know how many nights I could go without sleep.

A wave of cold air hit me as I unlocked my store. "Jeff, what did I tell you about the thermostat?"

My only employee shrugged his rounded shoulders from behind the counter without looking up from his game. "The server was getting hot."

Sometimes, I wondered why I kept him around.

He smiled, showing his straight, upper teeth. His bottom teeth looked like a traffic accident, so, he always kept them hidden with his lower lip. I tried to convince him no one cared about crooked teeth once you were older than twenty-two, but he remained super sensitive to the perceived flaw. If he was so worried about the way he appeared to other people, you'd think he'd dress in something other than old video game and band T-shirts.

As I passed Jeff to drop my purse in the back, my muscles tingled in a gentle, soothing way. Most men would be stressed out with the recent fight with his wife, but Jeff radiated contentment. Now I remembered why I kept him. His emotions were so mellow, it was like working with an android, which suited me just fine. Of course, that also might have been why he routinely found himself out of the house. Who was I to judge? I hadn't had a steady relationship since college and had no intention of changing that streak.

When I hit the threshold between the floor and the back room, crumbs littered the area and were ground into the carpet. Behind me, I tracked the trail of crackers to the register where Jeff shoved another in his mouth with one hand and maneuvered his avatar on screen with another.

Now that I noticed the mess, I couldn't see anything but the disaster. "Seriously?"

He looked up at me, the picture of innocence.

I shook my head as I grabbed the vacuum. "I'm starting to relate to your wife."

"Sorry." Jeff mumbled as he brushed crumbs from the counter to the floor.

He was so lucky I liked cleaning. It was therapeutic. A way to control my world when my curse overwhelmed me. The hum of the machine as it sucked up the crumbs and other miscellaneous dust provided just enough white noise for me to think. It was surreal that Albert Johnson, the Collector, was murdered before I even knew of his existence. The artist called to me from his work. I answered, but now he was gone. What kind of cruel trick was that? Who was in charge of this nonsense? I'd like to have a word.

With the worn-out carpet clean and Jeff emptying the bin, I hovered over the voicemail button on the phone. My elbow hit the desk as a noise from Jeff's video game surprised me. The laptop flashed, asking if Jeff wanted to play another round. He probably did, but he had work to do. I wished the store was bustling with customers to keep my mind focused on something besides Albert Johnson. If he was like me, there had to be others, right?

In a moment of absolute clarity, I closed Jeff's game and pulled up Google. I hadn't found anything about Albert Johnson, but maybe if I searched for the Collector, I might have better luck.

As soon as I hit enter, a whole world popped onto my screen. Reviews praised his innovative, experimental process. The Collector got his name because he went to estate sales all over Texas and found unique items to create his art. Though no article mentioned it, I knew that must be how he found the emotional remnants. For the same reason I avoided antiquing, Albert immersed himself in that world. I couldn't imagine subjecting yourself to such turmoil all the time. How had he centered himself? My mother's singing voice only worked for so long. Alcohol only numbed it. What was his trick?

His deep brown eyes danced with joy in each picture as he pointed out different pieces in his amalgamations. He didn't seem to have any compunction about touching any of it. How did he do that? A lump formed in my throat. I would never get to ask him.

Tight dreads framed his chiseled, golden-brown face. My mind superimposed his death mask of washed out skin and blood-soaked hair. Unable to see anything else, I stood up and grabbed the duster.

When my mind was back under control and the display monitors gleamed in the filtered light, I returned to the search. I wasn't about to give up. The store might end up cleaner than when I first moved in, but I would find answers.

A few more clicks took me to an events page. The Collector hosted a show at the Loblolly Gallery on Montrose Saturday night. That's the night Flores asked me about. Was he killed after his show? My curiosity compelled me to learn all I could. I didn't know how long galleries kept art after a show, but maybe someone there saw something weird. What could it hurt to check it out?

My stomach growled, reminding me I hadn't eaten anything since yesterday afternoon. "Jeff, do you want to GrubHub something?"

"Sure," he called from the employee restroom.

I closed the laptop and went into the back. The "break room," as we liked to call it, was through a door next to back storage. It had a little table with a couple of folding chairs, a hot plate, a full-sized fridge and sink, and a cot that Jeff called his second home. The old socks smell attested to the regularity.

"I'll order the food while you clean this up." I grabbed a Diet Dr. Pepper from the fridge while I scrolled the cheapest selections for the day.

The bell at the door rang, announcing a customer. Time to pay the rent.

At the counter stood a young man, maybe early twenties, with an average white-guy haircut and average white-guy jeans. He set down a laptop and drummed on its surface as he looked behind the counter like someone was hiding behind it.

"Can I help you?"

My question startled him, but he recovered quickly. "Yeah, I'm locked out of my stupid computer. Can you help me get in?"

Dammit. I hate these jobs. "Sometimes I can. It'll cost you $50 for the analysis."

"No problem. You'd be saving my butt." He pulled out his wallet and dropped a fifty-dollar bill on the counter.

I set my soda down maybe a bit too hard. Usually people complain about how much everything cost. Dropping that much cash without blinking an eye for a guy his age made me suspicious. It wouldn't be my first stolen laptop. Well, some good had to come from this curse, right? I took my gloves off and opened the laptop. The screen flashed to wallpaper of two toddlers.

I cocked my head at the twins that shared zero resemblance with the customer. "Cute kids."

The guy's face flushed red. "Their mom thinks so. This thing used to be my sister's, which is why it's probably cursed."

He didn't have a clue what that word really meant. "I'll see what I can do." I held out my hand to shake his.

When his skin touched mine, my eye twitched and my esophagus burned like I'd eaten a habanero, seeds and all. I couldn't read his mind. That wasn't part of my ability, but my body reacted in predictable ways to others' emotions. Over the years, I'd learned what each sensation meant. This customer was nervous and suffered from a heavy sense of guilt. Now that didn't mean for sure that he'd stolen the laptop. I was positive about his feelings, but couldn't necessarily discern their source. Nevertheless, this wasn't my first rodeo.

My gloves slipped on easily as he stared at my odd behavior. "I just need to make a phone call first," I said.

"For why?"

"I always report stolen goods." The old-fashioned receiver felt cold and refreshing against my ear.

"But...I..." he stammered as he considered the door, then the laptop, then the door again.

I slipped the computer under the counter as an authoritative female voice answered on the other end. "HPD, how may I assist you today?"

"Yes. I'd like to report a theft."

That was it. He took off out the front door, almost losing a shoe as the carpet transformed to cement under his feet.

Amelia laughed on the other end of the phone. "Did you catch another one?"

"I did. Thank you for being my officer-in-waiting."

"Anytime. Even though I don't know how you can always tell." Amelia's voice brought me peace. I wanted to confess all of the things that happened since we went shopping. Was that just two days ago?

"We all have our burdens to bear." More than I could even explain.

She chuckled. "Speaking of burdens, Gina's driving me nuts about Wednesday. Are you feeling well enough to go?"

"Much better." Which was a total lie, but some shots and a hot guy to make me forget about Albert Johnson sounded like a little touch of heaven. "It's scheduled and non-negotiable."

"Good." I didn't need the curse to tell Amelia sounded skeptical. "Gina's ready for one last school night party before returning to the land of the second graders when school starts."

"I'll text so she'll leave you alone." My gloved hands rubbed the warm laptop. "First, I need to find out who this laptop really belongs to."

"Talk at ya later."

As I hung up my work phone, I noticed the $50 bill still on the counter.

"Lunch is on me!" I shouted to Jeff in the back.

After ordering, I dug through the all-the-cords drawer. I'm sure I had a plug that would work for this model. The back of my hand stifled a yawn. The pop of the soda can promised a dose of caffeine to get me through until lunch arrived. The stolen laptop had an admin password of admin. Amateurs. With little effort, I found the owner's phone number and called her to come pick it up. She was so excited she said she'd send her brother, Tucker, to come get it since he worked close to the store. Maybe I did have superpowers.

When I hung up, a popup notice flashed from Jeff's laptop. I'd left it open on the gallery page. The ad announced the tragic death of the Collector and the auction of his last pieces Tuesday night. That was today. I'd spent the last dime I didn't have on that blasted statue, but I had to know everything I could about Albert Johnson.

I hadn't heard a thing from Detective Flores today. It was time to do some of my own investigating, but I didn't want to go alone. Amelia would hate a stuffy art exhibit. Gina might get a kick out of it though.

A few texts back and forth later, I had a date. Gina would come with me to the gallery tonight. It wouldn't be weird at all to show up after having found the man's dead body, now would it? I mean, who would know anyway?

To get my mind off the ridiculous decision I was probably making, I pulled up the customer tickets and got to work.

The rest of the afternoon flew by as the high from helping someone carried through the next job of reinstalling the operating system of a college student's virus-laden laptop. I had to find a way to show the kid how to surf the net for porn without killing his machine. If only his mom hadn't dropped it off for him.

Jeff waved goodnight to me before I realized it was closing

time. The clock on the laptop said it was 5:30pm. I needed to book it if I was going to get ready in time for the auction. Surely, I should wear something more formal than my Chipped polo and a pair of khakis.

I followed Jeff to the door. "Good luck with Linda tonight. Bring her some flowers or something."

He shrugged as he unlocked his late model Nissan. "They just make her sneeze."

Poor Jeff, I thought as I put the key in the door lock.

A man's voice called from the open door of a royal blue Audi S5 coupe. "Wait. Don't close yet please. My sister will kill me."

My shoulders tensed, and I thought about ignoring his call. Then the word "sister" registered, and I realized who he must have been. "Tucker, I assume?"

"Yes, ma'am. I'm sorry I couldn't get out of work any sooner," said the disembodied voice.

Dammit, I'd completely forgotten about the stolen computer. With a twist of the key in the opposite direction, I yanked the door open and waved the guy in behind me. "Let's make it quick. I've got somewhere to be."

I was behind the counter before the doorbell chimed on his entrance.

"Thank you for this. My sister has been livid about that laptop."

"No worries," I replied, even though I considered that old saying no good deed goes unpunished. I unplugged the laptop in question and stood up. "Can I see some ID? I don't want to hand it over to..."

My brain forgot how to words as it tried to translate the vision before me into reality. Tucker reached for the wallet in the front pocket of his scrubs while I tried to catch my breath. His straw-colored hair, short in back and long on top, begged me to run my fingers through it. His nose might have been called obtuse except for its strong masculine effect on his softly rounded cheeks and flawless warm ivory skin. When he looked up, with his eyes as blue as the mountain sky, I had to bite my lip to make sure my mouth wasn't hanging open.

"Are you okay?" he asked as he waved his license at me.

My eyes blinked as I resisted the urge to shake my head to clear it. As I studied his Texas driver's license, I was relieved he couldn't sense *my* emotions. "Tucker Wickman. As expected."

"Thanks again," he said as he accepted his sister's laptop. Then he offered me a folded-up bill. "And please take this for your trouble."

Well, that snapped me out of my trance. "No, no, no. It was my pleasure. Just remember Chipped if you have any tech issues."

His eyebrows crinkled and his lips parted in a sweet smile that formed a perfect little dimple in his left cheek. "We will."

He sort of saluted as he rushed out the door.

Wow. What was that? I gave him a moment to drive off before I headed out myself. I couldn't remember ever reacting to a man like that while sober. I must have been weak from the emotional up and down of the last few days.

And here I was about to torture myself more by hitting that gallery. Yet, I had to know. I'd lived through emotional turmoil before and never for a better reason than discovering answers about this curse. It was time to take a chance.

Chapter Nine

Through the open gallery door, the murmur of the well-dressed crowd bounced off the empty walls as Gina and I waited to be let in. Hesitant to be tormented by waves of impressions in the air, I smoothed my thin black dress with my velvet black-gloved hands. Usually I wore this dress out clubbing, the one place I didn't wear gloves. Yet, tonight I suspected I'd be surrounded by statues like Walter and people I might accidentally touch. I hadn't wanted to fight both of these attacks on my sanity simultaneously, so I scrounged around the back of my closet for something more protective and found the gloves I'd worn to my mother's funeral. I had no idea why I'd kept them, and they were much too warm for the setting, but it was better than nothing. I wasn't sure how much I'd learn if I was drunk before attending the auction, and that was my only other option, the only thing that kept the curse quiet so I could relax around people.

My stomach twisted and turned as the tuxedo at the door handed Gina and I paddles with numbers on them. I almost handed it back—I didn't have anything left after purchasing Walter—but I had to blend in if I was going to find any answers. With my tongue between my teeth, prepared for the onslaught of emotions, I breached the barrier between the outside and the gallery floor.

The Loblolly Gallery had floor to ceiling white walls and polished cement floors. The entire place was a blank canvas awaiting art to bring it to life. The track lighting offered the most movement with multiple possible positions, depending on what needed to be highlighted. At the moment, a couple walls had floral oil paintings, but the majority of the space was filled with Collector statues and incredibly well-dressed patrons.

Oh no, I couldn't face the attack of all of these creations. I'd pass out right in front of all these people. I stepped back and almost ran into Gina.

"Where are you going?" she asked. "This stuff is amazing. It's like the statue you paid a crazy amount for."

Her red, floor length dress clung to her petite frame, the only fold a slight cheat at her chest to imitate the curves she didn't have. Her four-inch heels, which elevated her to my height, clicked delicately on the concrete floor as she practically dragged me to the nearest piece. I envied her light step when my heavy feet sounded like clogs. Luckily, the crowd absorbed the sound by sheer density. However, that same density offered threats of its own. I pressed the paddle against my chest to make sure I didn't touch anyone.

Then I realized, I was fine. The crowd exuded a mixed bag, though it was all pretty muted. As I passed different mingling groups, my body was treated to sensations instead of being assaulted by them. Apparently, this particular gathering had learned to control their emotions. If I was in charge, that skill would be taught in school. My life would be so much smoother then.

As for the art, the air didn't vibrate with the energy of connected impressions like it had at Finishing Touches or in my living room if I took the layers of blankets off Walter. Were these statues made of normal junk instead of remnants? What if

Walter was the only piece Albert had ever made of a full conglomeration?

If that was true, why would he have so many individual pieces stored at his condo? I was supposed to be finding answers, not more questions. It was time to suck it up and see if any of these statues called to the cursed.

There was a tingling as I approached the piece Gina gawked at. So, there was definitely at least *an* impression tied into it. I leaned toward the creation of a dolphin arching through a wave. Driftwood and broken glass and pieces of old wire were all connected in a swirl to imitate movement in the water. The sea animal itself looked to be an old piece of crystal. Oddly enough, the emotional remnant didn't seem to vibrate from the dolphin, but from the carved rock sticking out of the water underneath it. I couldn't tell what the memory held, but after what I'd experienced the last two days, I didn't want to chance a closer inspection. I didn't hear his voice either, the one that sent me to his apartment.

Gina's tight, dancer's bun didn't move as she cocked her head at me. I just knew she was trying to read my mind. It wasn't the first time I'd seen that look. "Why did you want to come to this event again?" She waved a hand at the milling audience. "You usually make fun of me for my appreciation of the arts."

I wished I could tell her the truth. If I confessed, she'd immediately drag me out of here and call Amelia. I did not push myself this far outside my comfort zone to walk away empty-handed. "Okay. Full confession. I looked up the artist, Albert Johnson. He was so good-looking I *had* to meet him."

Gina's hip cocked the opposite direction of her head and I knew I had her. "But isn't he, like, dead?" The last word slipped out in a whisper.

I led her away from the stares that turned in our direction. "Which is why I had to come see his final pieces. I don't know why, but I felt an immediate connection with Albert Johnson, the Collector. I wasn't ready to let that go." To my own surprise, a tear escaped my eye as the truth in those words struck deeper than I'd intended. At least, this was *my* emotion.

"Oh, Fauna, I'm so sorry. I didn't know you felt so much for his art." Gina retrieved a tissue from her purse and gently patted my cheek of moisture.

I didn't flinch. Her concern warmed the cold emptiness of the loss I hadn't expected to feel. After all, I hadn't even met the guy. "Want to keep browsing?"

"Of course." Gina squeezed my gloved hand and then let go. I could see her reluctance to do so, but she knew I didn't like to be touched.

Everyone should have a friend like Gina.

As we cruised through the exhibit, each piece was wholly unique while still obviously connected to the mind of one artist. Even for people who couldn't sense the impressions, I understood their appeal. My mood depressed as I realized the loss of this artist wasn't just on me but on the community. He made beauty by adding life to dead and useless things. Even more reason to find his murderer and bring him to justice.

Every statue we came across had one section I could sense was a remnant, but none of them called to me in Albert's voice. I wondered if he had found another method to find other cursed people. Or if he never found any others and gave up. The back of my eyes started to throb. Someone nearby was feeling the same sort of sadness. I needed something to drink or all of these people so close together was going to force me out.

"Let's head to the bar." I gestured toward the cart set up next to the desk near the front.

Gina perked up. "Yes, please."

The very pretty bartender with his shiny almond skin, high cheek bones, and contagious smile made me feel better as soon as I set my card on the bar top. "Two margaritas please. Easy on the mix, heavy on the Cointreau."

Gina raised a delicate finger. "No salt for me please."

"Yes, ma'am," he practically sang the lines. I wondered if he had show experience. I could see the pretty boy on the stage garnering the attention of the entire audience whenever he opened his mouth. "Would you like to keep a tab open?"

Gina and I replied simultaneously. "Yes."

While we sipped our drink, I searched the crowd wondering if I was really going to find out anything else or if I was wasting my time. I wasn't sure what to look for. I was great at troubleshooting—fixing a misbehaving laptop or a behind-in-updates cell phone—but investigating was beyond my skill set.

As if the word summoned him, I spotted Detective Flores with an elderly woman, who couldn't have weighed more than a cat. Her remarkably thick mop of gray hair was piled on her head, held back with pins that were pieces of modern art. Her clothes hung from her petite frame, looking as comfortable as a bathrobe though in much more expensive fabrics. She looked distracted and rather annoyed until a tall, handsome gentleman interrupted the detective.

The older woman smiled with a welcoming look as she tried to shoulder Flores from her immediate vicinity. To his credit, the detective simply offered his hand to the man who shook it back with a large rubied ring prominent on his finger. I cocked my head at the handsome middle-aged man. I was pretty sure it was the same guy from the precinct Monday. I guess it made sense for Albert's fans to be in both places.

Before Flores spotted me, I took advantage of the tailored guy's distraction to steer Gina toward the door. "You know, I don't know what I was thinking. You're right I can't afford a thing here. Let's go get some tacos and call it a night." The last thing I needed was more suspicion aimed at me.

Surprise blossomed on Gina's face. "Seriously? But we just got here. And you haven't closed out your tab."

"Dammit." I positioned my body awkwardly for the bartender but at the best angle I could get to avoid eye contact with Flores.

As I waved to the bartender for my card, my abdomen

cramped so fiercely, I involuntarily bent over. This anger seemed out of place among the sedate crowd. The fury of Albert's murderer flashed through my mind, and I almost vomited on the concrete floor.

Thank god for Gina. "Oh, you do look a little green." She took my purse and put my card from the bartender in it.

When she wrapped her free hand around my waist to guide me toward the door, I couldn't move. I had to know if the murderer had entered. With a calming breath in and out, my mom's hymn eased the pain in my gut.

"Just one more thing," I managed to say.

Without a clue of what excuse I'd give Gina and without any concern for Flores spotting me, I slowly turned to follow the trail of anger.

A tall man, in business attire much too casual for this fancy event, carried a large package wrapped in butcher paper to the front desk. His face was flushed, but I doubted it was from exertion, because he looked to be in good shape. His dark hair and light blue eyes sent renewed shivers through me. I still hadn't been able to piece together an accurate image of Albert's murderer, but these preliminary clues fit.

"Wow," Gina said beside me. "I can see why you're feeling better. Shall I leave you two alone?"

Fear flushed my skin at the thought of being alone with the angry man. "No," I retorted.

Maybe a bit too harshly, because Gina crossed her arms just like Amelia always did when she was calling me on my shit.

"I'm sorry," I quickly added. "I'm curious about what he brought to a gallery in the middle of an auction."

"Hmph." Gina turned, pulled my card back out, and ordered another drink from the bartender.

Relieved that I'd avoided one crisis, I moved closer to the desk to verify my suspicions. Anxiety tried to freeze my feet, but logic reassured me that he wouldn't attack me in front of all these people.

The numbered paddle pushed air around my face as I subconsciously used it like a fan. If I could get him to roll up his sleeves, I'd know for sure. Those scars from Albert's memory were unmistakable.

Gina startled me with an offer of another drink. Her cheery smile was back on her face. She was so understanding with my mood swings. If I discovered nothing with this little field trip, I'd have wasted her time and used her friendship. And she didn't even know why we were here.

With a shaky hand, I took a generous sip on the tart margarita. A drip spilled on my glove and wicked off the velvet. That gave me a brilliant idea for catching a glimpse of the angry man's arms. In an exaggerated slip, I spilled the rest of my drink on his long-sleeved shirt.

Chapter Ten

He yelled and jumped back a step. "What are you doing, you clumsy drunk?"

His ire punched my gut as if he'd actually hit me. The pain was so intense I feared my intestines had ruptured.

Gina stepped in and pulled a cloth from her bag to pat at his arm. "I'm so sorry, sir. My friend's not feeling well."

She seemed to have whatever was needed in that bag. Her penchant for preparedness came in handy; this time more than most. Before he yanked his arm from her, I got a good look at his forearm as the liquid made the white material translucent. Smooth, unblemished skin brushed against the sticky, salty stain. The only damage I could pick out was bruising on the knuckles of his right hand. That could be from anything.

An odd mix of disappointment and relief washed through me which helped to unclench my stomach. I certainly had no intention of confronting a killer, but I had hoped to solve this mystery and bring Albert's murderer to justice.

In my steady, sober voice, I pulled Angry Man's attention from Gina. "I apologize, sir. These are new heels and I'm afraid they don't fit quite right. May I buy you a drink as an apology?"

"No." His definitive answer and haunting blue eyes told me

the man was beyond reason. He might not be the murderer, but I could feel violence in his movements.

Gina stared at my feet with obvious confusion on her face. Then she met my eye with an almost Amelia accusation. She knew I was lying and that I'd spilled that drink on purpose. Crap. Now I had to come up with some sort of explanation.

The older lady excused herself from Detective Flores and made her way to the register. Before I could figure out how to hide, Flores made eye contact with me. His instant scowl made him look like my high school principal about to chastise me for being in the hallway between classes.

I wasn't ready for this. How guilty must I have looked having found a murder victim—whom I claimed to not know—then showing up a couple days later at an event held for the same man. I knew Collins already suspected me of being involved. And here I was, verifying his doubts of my innocence. Well, it was too late to turn back now. I might as well learn what I could.

As the older woman sorted herself behind the counter, I realized she wore a lanyard around her neck with her name: "Rhonda Turgerson, Owner."

She must have known Albert. She was hosting his show and now a benefit after his death. Maybe she could tell me something else about him.

Her voice sounded quiet, but authoritative. "What can I help you with, Mr. Elstin? We are about to start the auction, if you'd like to have a seat."

"I don't want any of that man's garbage in my house." The angry man stretched his neck and stood over the petite woman as much as he could from the other side of the counter. "I wish to consign this piece to the auction. It should be worth a pretty penny since he's dead."

"That's a very interesting statement." To her credit, Mrs. Turgerson didn't look a bit cowed by his aggressive demands. She gently unwrapped the thick paper and plastic covering the piece. "How is your fist doing?"

Detective Flores, who stood close to the counter seemingly paying no attention to what was going on, perked up and glanced down at the man's bruised hand. Turgerson nodded at Flores's lifted eyebrow.

Interesting. They knew something I didn't. Well, they probably knew a lot of things I didn't. I needed to get Mrs. Turgerson alone and see if I could gleam anything from her. I wondered if she knew of Albert's curse.

Then his voice drifted up from the statue. It sounded more ghostly to me than it had the first time I heard it in the small shop. *Don't fight it. Embrace your gift and come find me.* So, the statues I was able to get close to in this exhibit didn't have his voice, but the one Angry Man Elstin returned did.

More clues; still zero answers.

"I'm sorry, Mr. Elstin." Mrs. Turgerson flipped through a book and placed her finger on an entry. "According to our records, this particular art belongs to Dr. Debra Elstin. I'm afraid if I purchased it from you, your wife could report it as stolen goods. I will not risk my impeccable reputation."

Mr. Elstin slammed his hand on the counter. "It's not stolen. It's ours. It sat in our living room taunting me."

Flores casually adjusted his lanyard with his badge. "What happened to your hand, Mr. Elstin?"

After shoving his hands in his pocket, Mr. Elstin took a step back from the counter. "What are you suggesting?" His eyes went from the stoic Mrs. Turgerson to the calm Detective Flores. "He deserved it. He was fucking my wife. I didn't kill him, but I'm certainly not upset he's dead."

His loud statement muffled the crowd better than any gavel on an auction block. In my mind, I raised the volume of my mom's voice. I had to stifle the cramping in my gut by warding as much of his anger as possible. I was *not* running away in pain when I was about to learn more about Albert.

With all eyes looking our way, Mrs. Turgerson calmly re-wrapped the statue. "I will call Dr. Elstin to pick up her property." Having dismissed Mr. Elstin, she turned to Flores. "If I think of anything else, I'll be sure to give you a call, Detective."

Man, I had to hand it to her. That woman was queen of her kingdom and she knew how to wield that power.

"Thank you, ma'am." Detective Flores motioned Mr. Elstin toward the door. "Let's take this outside."

Mr. Elstin hesitated. "But, my property?"

Flores herded Mr. Elstin to the front door simply by walking toward him. "Well, according to Mrs. Turgerson's records, that's stolen property."

Collins's voice behind me startled me into Gina. "Stolen property? Let's take it down to the precinct and get it all straightened out." He brandished his hand cuffs like he was checking for the time on his watch.

Flores had a quiet authority about him, like a stern dad you didn't want to disappoint. Collins, on the other hand, felt like the Harvey Dent in this partnership. I could picture him getting a confession with his fists.

The crowd murmurs picked up again. Though I suspected this time, it had little to do with the art and much more to do with the current dramatic performance. This could be my chance to talk to Mrs. Turgerson. Or if I could get to her computer, I could get information on Dr. Debra Elstin. If she was having an affair with Albert, she might have more answers for me. After all, she had one of his statues that called out to cursed people. It couldn't just be a coincidence, right?

Cursed people. I can't believe I just thought that. There really could be more of us.

As Collins took control of escorting Mr. Elstin out the door, Flores turned his attention to me.

"No, dammit." My foot tapped on the floor.

"What?" Gina watched Flores approaching with her head tilted. My nipples tingled at Gina's lustful feelings. "I mean, I'll talk to him if you don't want to."

If only she knew the truth. I really should've told her. My

mind swam in circles as Flores approached. I had other things to worry about right now, like staying involved without becoming a stronger suspect. "Detective Flores." *So witty of me.*

"Ms. Young." Flores put his hands in the pockets of his slacks.

The badge around his neck bounced as his chest flexed under his smartly ironed shirt. I wouldn't want to arm wrestle the man. I wondered if I'd have any better luck trying to outmaneuver him. So far, not so good.

His accusatory look made me feel I needed to defend myself. "I'm allowed to be here."

"How did you find this place?"

I cocked my head. His suspicions were starting to annoy me. "Um, in the modern world they have this thing called the internet. I searched for the Collector and voilà, the auction popped up."

"And you didn't think to come here first instead of his apartment in the middle of the night?" His phone re-appeared in his hand as he jotted down more notes.

My balance shifted from foot to foot as I fought the urge to run away. "I only knew him as Albert Johnson. I didn't know he was called the Collector until..." *Until you told me at the scene.* This whole damn thing sounded suspicious to me too.

Flores continued, "So, you weren't here at the show on Saturday?"

My arms folded against my chest as my anger rose. "I already told you I was out with friends and gave you their info."

Gina raised her hand beside me. "I have no idea what's going on," her pointed look told me she expected to be filled in later, "but, I happen to be one of those friends, and we were out clubbing until almost midnight."

Flores turned his deep brown eyes to my friend. "And your name is?"

"Gina Nguyen."

His fingers flew over his phone. I had to come up with a

reason to still be interested in this case. I couldn't very well tell Flores the artist was cursed like me, and I couldn't walk away until I learned everything I could.

"Look. I'm the one who found him and now I feel responsible for finding who did it."

Flores's dark eyes studied me though his face still angled down toward his phone. "That's *my* job."

"Well…" I had no idea what to say. My stomach rumbled with anxiety.

Mrs. Turgerson startled me when she spoke from my side. Man, I was jumpy today. "We're about to begin, Detective. If you don't mind?" She indicated the door with a slight tilt of her head and a raised eyebrow.

Flores tucked his phone into his jacket. "Of course, Mrs. Turgerson. Before I go, I want to verify that Mr. Elstin is the man you said punched Albert Johnson Saturday night."

She nodded. "Ted will send over the surveillance video to the email you gave me after we've concluded the auction. He's busy organizing the online portion of the show."

Flores's shoulders tensed. I didn't feel anything in the air around him. It was almost like going blind. I couldn't guess what he felt about me as a suspect or the case at all. He had to be used to keeping everything tightly under control.

"Thank you, Mrs. Turgerson."

His tone made me picture a cowboy in an old western. I half expected him to touch his non-existent ten-gallon hat as he made for the door. As he opened it, I fell into my old enemy—indecision. Should I rush after him and try and convince him to keep me in the loop or stay behind and try to get information out of Mrs. Turgerson? One look at the older woman's face told me that was a no-go. Flores, at least, had suspicions about my involvement. Maybe he'd keep me close to simply learn more about what I knew?

Gina tapped me on my gloved hand. "What was that all about?"

I blinked at her like I'd forgotten she was there, which maybe I had a little. I was a horrible friend. "I'm sorry, Gina. I have to ask that detective something."

My heels clipped on the floor as I rushed to catch up to Flores. Without turning around to see Gina, I knew she was pissed when I heard her glass hit the bar top a bit too roughly as she asked for the card back again. I'd make it up to her later.

Flores held the door open for me as if he'd never stopped watching me. In the parking lot, Collins talked to Elstin next to a marked car. The suspect wasn't cuffed yet, but Collins still held the metal restraints in his hand.

"This is bullshit," Angry Man Elstin blustered. "I didn't do anything. The Collector was the jerk. Have you checked all of his other customers' husbands? There's probably a long list of families he destroyed."

Collins seemed to side with Elstin, though he never stopped swinging the cuffs in his fingers. "Artists, right? They think because they play like kindergarteners all day, that makes them irresistible."

Elstin sneered. "Exactly. And this Albert guy was the worst. After my wife brought home that ugly piece of shit, she was obsessed with the man. I know they were meeting secretly. I followed them one night and she left her car at his condo and got into his."

Collins snorted. "Naturally, they went to a hotel, didn't they?"

Flores had taken out his phone and started taking notes. I swore he was paying more attention to me than Elstin though.

"Oh, they definitely did, but I lost them and didn't see which one." Elstin waved at the gallery. "So, I followed her to his show and confronted him. When he smugly denied everything, I lost it." His hands clenched in fists. "But I didn't kill him."

Collins dismissed the possibility with a wave of his hand. "Of course not, because you have an alibi. I'm sure you and the missus went home to air out your grievances and make up."

Elstin's jerky motions ceased, as he looked up with fear in his eyes. "Not exactly. We drove in separate cars and Debra refused to answer her phone. She didn't come home that night at all."

Flores said next to me. "Do you recognize him from anywhere?"

He wanted to know if I'd seen Elstin that night? I wondered if that cleared me as a suspect in his eyes. "He doesn't have the scars on his arms."

His scrunched eyes at my answer left me doubting my own conclusions.

Luckily, Gina came out and shoved my purse against my chest to save me from melting under Flores's scrutiny.

Collins turned Elstin around to get the cuffs on him. "Maybe you did; maybe you didn't. We'll work it all out downtown."

Elstin's bluster faded. "Why? I told you everything."

"You did." Collins nodded as the uniformed office tucked Elstin into the back seat of his squad car. "You told us you have motive, knew where the guy lived, and have no alibi for the night in question."

As the squad car pulled away, Collins turned to Flores and cracked his knuckles. "Are we taking anyone else in?"

Without looking back at me, Flores shook his head. "That's it for today."

As the detectives pulled away in their navy blue Ford Fusion, my mind swam with helplessness again. Gina didn't let me dwell there for long though.

She whipped me around by my elbow. "What is going on?"

I rubbed the velvet of my long glove over my forehead. There was no keeping her out of it, and when I told her Amelia would know too. I might as well tell them both at once. "Let's call Amelia. There's something I need to tell you both."

Chapter Eleven

O ur favorite late-night diner was Kenny and Ziggy's out by the Galleria. Though technically not late yet, I thought meeting here would remind Gina and Amelia what good friends we were. Hopefully, they wouldn't be too angry that I hadn't told them what I'd seen Sunday or that I'd been keeping a secret from them all these years.

I munched a fresh pickle out of a tiny bowl to keep my eyes anywhere but on Gina. Not that I could see her face right now, since she was buried in the plastic menu the size of a yearbook.

I tried to lighten the mood. "You already know what you're ordering." If Gina Nguyen ordered anything besides the Swiss and Shout—basically a Reuben but with turkey pastrami—the world would probably come to an end. Though the humungous portions meant she only nibbled a bit and took the rest home. I'd be willing to bet it fed her all week.

"Hmph," was all she said.

I preferred to explore the menu. Cooking was one of my outlets, the way I could express my love for my friends. Since I avoided touching them, hugs were rare. I could, however, fill their plates with homemade goodness or surprise them at work with a hot plate of food.

Right now, I think I needed something warm and comforting. I hadn't opened up like I planned to do now since my mother died. The velvet of the same gloves I wore to that event suddenly felt oppressive, even in the air-conditioned space. I took them off and set them in my lap.

Gina peered to the side of the menu at me.

I had to say something. "Look. I'm sorry. As soon as Amelia—"

"As soon as Amelia what?"

I jumped as Amelia's presence filled the space right before her body did. She moved past me and sat beside Gina who folded the menu and her arms in one smooth movement.

"Uh oh, I missed something." Amelia waved over Stella, our regular waitress. I didn't know if that was her real name or if she was just living up to the New York accent she affected. Again, I didn't know if that was real or part of the act either, but we loved her just the same.

As Stella bent over to drop off a fresh bowl of pickles, her chest practically touched the table. Everything about her was petite, her height, her waist, her tiny hands, and button nose, except for her gray-streaked hair. Always pulled back in a ponytail, it swayed all the way down passed the tie of her apron.

"What can I get you girls tonight?" Stella cocked her hip and pointed her pen at Amelia. "When you came in, I had to check the calendar to make sure it wasn't Wednesday or Saturday."

This was turning out to be anything but an ordinary week. "Gina and I went to an art show tonight."

Stella whistled and motioned to the TV over the deli counter. "Did you see that poor artist who was murdered in his home this weekend? It's just not safe out there."

"You know, I *hadn't* heard of a murdered artist *until* we arrived at the art show. If only we'd gone to look at the art, it might have been fun." Gina handed her menu over to Stella. "I'll have a slice of strawberry cheesecake please."

Uh oh, maybe the world was coming to an end.

"Whew." Amelia's face opened in surprise. "I don't think I've ever seen you eat dessert here."

With her arms re-crossed, Gina responded, "I've never been confronted by policemen while out with my friend either."

How much was I going to confess? Obviously, I had to tell them that I found Albert, but what about the curse? I couldn't lose them. They were my only family.

Stella's raised eyebrow reminded me she needed my order. The lump in my throat blocked anything from coming out. Instead, I pointed to the matzah soup.

"One matzah soup. And for you?" She turned to Amelia.

"Well, in this topsy turvy world, I guess I'll have Schmutzy fries."

With the menus in hand and the promise of more water on her return, Stella swung her hips to the kitchen.

Gina and Amelia both turned their eyes to me. Gina waiting for my confessions. Amelia waiting for an explanation. My fingers kneaded the gloves in my lap. These two were my oldest friends. They'd stuck with me through all kinds of quirky things and accepted my lame excuses or got by on nothing at all. They never judged me or questioned me. And I'd never been honest with them. I could at least come clean about what I'd seen Sunday night.

Amelia broke the silence. She never could stand to stay quiet for long. "Okay. First, I'm so grateful you two didn't drag me to something as boring as looking at art, but—"

"Oh, it wasn't boring." Gina took a violent sip of her water, splashing a bit on the table. Usually, the mess would drive her crazy. She ignored it. "Some angry guy showed up and Fauna spilled her drink on him *on purpose*."

I tried to interrupt, but Gina put a hand up to silence me.

"Then a police detective happened to be there and *knew* Fauna. I thought she was going to be arrested. Then Fauna called *him* by name." She shifted her focus to me. "You didn't seem surprised to see him, but you didn't give me a single heads up." A tear dropped down her round cheek. "I was so scared, and you would hardly look at me, and I didn't know what to do."

The last words came out as a whisper. I reached out and covered Gina's hand with my own. Her anxiety throbbed in my temples. What I had sensed as anger was really anxiety. Body language could be so confusing sometimes. No wonder I couldn't get through to her. I tried to make her forgive me instead of making her feel safe.

Amelia put her arm over Gina's shoulders, but her focus fell on me. "Okay. Your turn."

"I was surprised Detective Flores was at Albert Johnson's auction, but I shouldn't have been. I should have told you, Gina." I removed my hand from hers. It felt like such an invasion to read her emotions when I'd already kept things from her today.

Amelia pulled out a tissue from Gina's bag and handed it to her. "Isn't Albert Johnson that guy who made that horrible statue you bought Sunday?"

"He is, or was. He's the artist guy Stella was talking about. He was murdered that night."

After giving her nose a good swipe, Gina leaned forward. "You told me he died, but you didn't tell me he was murdered."

Always the logical one, Amelia angled her head at the TV. "If he was a murder victim, it explains why the cop was there." She leaned forward like Gina. "But it doesn't explain why he knew you."

I was being interrogated all over again. This time, I'd asked for it. "I tracked down Albert Johnson. There was something about the piece that really spoke to me. I just had to talk to the artist."

I shifted my glass from hand to hand to avoid looking them in the eyes. "I found his dead body on the floor of his kitchen."

Gina gasped and held her mouth with both hands.

Amelia's hand fell to the table, bouncing the bowl of pickles. "You what?"

"When I got to his condo and knocked, the door swung open." The memory of the dozens of remnants near the door inundating me with their imprints invaded my thoughts. What would they think if I told them everything? "I'm the one who called 911."

With her gaze focused on the table and her head shaking slightly, Amelia said, "But I talked to you Tuesday. You sounded, well, normal. You didn't say anything about finding a dead body."

"I know. I know." My head fell into my hands as the vinegar from the pickles soured in my stomach. "I hadn't quite processed it all yet."

"No. That's not good enough." Sensing calm and cool Gina freaking out hurt me physically. "There's something else you're not telling us. Otherwise, *why* would you drag me to the auction of the artist whose body you found?"

Maybe this was a horrible idea. I never should have involved her in any of this. "You're not wrong. There's definitely something I'm not telling you." My knees banged together under the table as sitting behind the booth became too confining. I longed to pace.

Obviously, tired of waiting for me to explain, Gina turned sideways to face Amelia directly. "That detective questioned Fauna like he thought she might have had something to do with the Collector's death. He no doubt suspected her of something."

My head shot up, and I waved my hands. "I had nothing to do with his death, I promise. I would never lie about something like that."

The rash move might have knocked my water glass if Amelia hadn't caught it. "Look, we know you're not violent. You almost had a heart attack when you accidentally hit that suicidal squirrel last year."

"There's something else though." I had to tell them. I couldn't give up searching for others with the curse now that I knew I wasn't the only one. Weird shit was going to keep happening and I couldn't keep it all from my best friends.

But if I confessed the true secret, would they believe me?

Stella gave me a bit more grace period when she brought our orders to the table. "Here ya go, ladies."

Her voice sounded off. When I looked up and reached for my bowl, I'd forgotten I didn't have my gloves on. My fingers brushed hers and all of my muscles squeezed at the same time. My jaw locked so hard I bit my tongue. Whatever had happened between Stella taking our orders and returning with them had sent the waitress into deep grief.

I swallowed heavily and blinked to force my muscles to unclench. "What's wrong, Stella?"

Her voice turned ragged as she barely handed over the last plate before she had to dive in her pocket for a napkin to blow her nose. "He's dead. I can't believe it. He was the best of the best. Even predicted my sister's cancer early and saved her life."

"Who?" I asked.

Stella turned to the TV over the deli.

A blonde anchor in a blue and orange dress reported, "Renowned Psychic, George Martinez, was murdered inside his home today. His body was discovered this evening. The police have no suspects at this time."

As the studio anchor droned on, a picture of a middle-aged man with pot-marked skin, deep brown eyes, and a fedora popped up beside her.

Holy shit. That was the man from the precinct who creeped me out. No wonder he looked familiar to me. He'd been on daytime TV more than once. Jeff said his wife followed everything the psychic did. Why had he given me that pointed stare Monday morning? Was Albert's death connected to this recent murder?

When I was younger and still searching for answers, I met as many mediums, psychics, and fortune tellers as I could. Not one could do what I could. After that, I'd written the whole community off as frauds. Maybe my exploring hadn't been extensive enough. What if George Martinez's reputation came from reading people's emotions? Holy shit, could he be cursed? How many of us were there?

The screen flipped to a reporter on a street I recognized in the Heights. The live feed showed police cars and yellow tape blocking off an area around a modest house. All of its lights were on like a beacon begging for help.

The smart-dressed female reporter spoke in the jilted, unnatural way required of newscasters. Her unemotional voice did nothing to calm the turmoil growing in my gut. "With no official statement from the police as of yet, our sources have told us that George Martinez was found in his home by his housekeeper with multiple stab wounds."

My fingers tingled at my fierce grip on the table. Could this be a coincidence?

Any doubt at the connection vanished when the camera zoomed in on the scene. In the front window stood one of the Collector's pieces.

Chapter Twelve

After lying to them before, I wasn't going to lie now. "I have to go to the scene."

Gina looked shocked. "Why?"

Amelia stood up to see the TV better. "That looks a lot like your statue, Fauna."

"It's definitely one of the Collector's. It has to be." I swallowed hard as the smells and sights of Albert lying on his kitchen floor flashed through my mind. Would those ever fade? "And they were both stabbed."

With hands on either side of her head, Gina rocked gently in her seat. "That's not okay. But you don't need to go. Let the cops handle it."

I shoved my velvet gloves back on my hand, all sign of an appetite gone. "You don't understand everything, and I don't even know where to begin, but I do know I *have* to go to the scene. I might be able to help."

The idea that I could help came out of my mouth before it had fully formed in my mind. If Detective Flores was there and I could convince him to let me in, maybe I could touch something and get a better look at the murderer. There was no such thing as coincidence, right? How many brilliant minds had repeated that mantra? Who was I to argue? If there were no coincidences, then these two with the same pieces of art, taken from the world by the same method, had to be connected. I promised Albert Johnson justice and I would *not* neglect my duty in achieving it.

My girlfriends stared at me as I pulled $60 from my wallet and put it on the table. "You two stay and eat. I'm going to call an Uber."

"Nice try." Amelia pulled her keys from her pocket. "If you're set on going, I'm taking you. I know there's something you're leaving out."

Gina pushed her plate back and scooted out of the booth seat. "I'm going too. You said there was one more thing. I want to hear it."

I grabbed the cash to leave at the register on our way out. "Okay, fine."

In the car, I sat in the back. Amelia kept glancing at me through the rearview mirror with her judgy eyes, while Gina put on lipstick and powdered her nose like she couldn't have her hands idol. I hadn't felt more like a child punished by her parents ever. My dad had died when I was too young to have a memory of him, and my mom treated me like I was her sister, not her daughter.

Dammit. I had to lie one more time. I feared I was getting good at it. "The last bit I left out, the part I was trying to get to, was I think I saw the killer fleeing the scene."

Gina dropped her lipstick. "You what?"

Amelia's eyes stared at the mirror a bit too long and she almost missed the turn.

I squeezed the seatbelt so I wouldn't slip into the door. "I don't *know* it was the killer. I mean, it was hours after Albert was already dead according to Detective Flores's check of my alibi. He'll probably be calling you later, Amelia." Yet, I did know it was the killer since I saw him stabbing Albert through the artist's last memory. How was I going to tell *that* to my friends? "But I did see a man run away as I entered Albert's building."

Gina nodded as she rocked gently in the passenger seat. "That explains the questions the detective asked. He wanted to know if you recognized that angry dude at the auction."

"Right." At least, Gina seemed satisfied. Amelia, though, had her lips so pierced that I wasn't sure words could escape if she wished to speak.

Flashing red and blue lights and a bright white one lit up a dark street we drove passed.

"There," I said, though Amelia must have seen it at the same time because she already had her blinker on to do a U-turn.

She pulled up next to the side street without turning into it. "Why don't you get out here?" Without even putting the car in park, Amelia crossed her arms and looked out the side window refusing to look at me.

The lights called to me, even as my conscience pulled at my conviction. "I'll see you guys tomorrow night."

"Wait, Fauna." Gina moved to unclick her seatbelt.

Amelia grabbed her hand and shook her head. "Let her go. She obviously has secrets she needs to tend to. You'll call an Uber home, right?"

Her eyes met mine and all I saw in their soft green tint was pain. She knew I was lying and was hurt.

"I'll get an Uber."

As my best friends drove off, I stalked to the crime scene. I'd make it up to them. If I just found the killer and cleaned up this whole affair, I could finally tell them the whole truth. If I found someone else with this curse, Amelia and Gina would be more likely to believe me, right?

The scene swarmed with reporters in front of cameras and officers in and out of the modest home. The statue of what looked like an elephant pieced together just like my Walter sat large and proud in the front window, like George Martinez also searched for others.

With one hand on a traffic cone, I wondered if I could sneak into the home to get a quick read on the place.

Of course, I might be seeing patterns where none existed. This murder might be a coincidence. It could have nothing to do with Albert at all. Or worse. Someone could be targeting us. Fear turned my empty stomach into a cauldron of acid.

I dismissed my paranoid musings. If I couldn't find other cursed people, how could a killer hunt us down? One way or another, I wouldn't learn anything if I couldn't get inside.

The police officer by the barrier yawned. I liked sleepy people. Their feelings tended to be muted.

"Excuse me, Officer?" I twirled my hair on my finger. A little flirting never hurt my cause before. "What happened? I was on my way home—I live right over there—and traffic stopped me cold." Shit, I really was getting good at this lying bit.

Officer Yawner perked up a bit as I batted my eyelashes at him. "I wasn't first on scene." He leaned in close, and my nipples perked. How was he feeling lustful at a murder scene? At least that was an emotion I could work with, while still in my slinky dress. "But I heard over the radio that George Martinez, the famous psychic, was stabbed to death in his own home."

A deep voice called from the front lawn. "Officer, bring her over here."

Around the big man's body, I spotted Detective Collins pointing at me. A flash of excitement rushed through me. Surely, the City of Houston had more than two homicide detectives. If he was here, that meant the two murders must be related, right?

I patted the uniformed officer with my protected hand, a bit of disappointment floated between us. A reporter tried to squeeze in behind me, but the cop stopped her with a smooth sidestep.

Collins met me in the middle of the street, hands on his hips, with a disappointed father look on his face. "It wasn't your voice on the 911 call this time. How are you connected to all of this?"

A quick glance of the general vicinity didn't reveal Flores anywhere. For some reason, I felt safer with him.

Collins's dark expression demanded an answer. "I saw the

Collector statue in the window and I had to know if..." *he was cursed too.*

He took my elbow and guided me toward the side of the house, out of the view of the cameras I suspected. "It's quite a coincidence that we run into you at the first victim's gallery auction and now, that same night, at a second victim's home." My stomach clenched, sensing the anger laced into his accusations.

I shook him off me. "Don't touch me."

With one hand on his belted cuffs, Collins's other hand flexed like he wanted to restrain me. "I will arrest you for interfering in an investigation. I don't care what Flores says. You're definitely hiding something."

"Fauna Young, what are you doing here?" Flores's voice turned both our heads to the back of the house.

That was when I saw through the brightly lit bedroom window.

Tied to the headboard and footboard, like some sort of sacrifice, laid the naked George Martinez.

The scene was much cleaner than Albert's murder. The mattress soaked up much of the blood and the walls were almost spotless. Either the murderer cleaned up after himself this time, or he took more care with much less chaotic violence. Nevertheless, the mutilation of the body was so extensive, it covered almost all the exposed skin on his torso. The weirdest part of the scene was George's face.

He was smiling.

The pickles swirling in my stomach threatened to come up.

Detective Collins answered for me. "Found her hanging back in the crowd. She was probably trying to figure out what we know."

My cheeks had to be bright red based on how warm they felt. I couldn't stop my hands from shaking as another gruesome scene burnt itself into my memory. Why was I fighting to experience this horror?

Flores's focus flicked between me and the window. He moved between me and the graphic scene and gestured toward the street. "I'm sure I'll have questions for you later, Ms. Young."

Collins scoffed and headed to the front door. "I don't know what you see that I don't, but she's your problem, man."

Flores motioned to a uniformed officer. "For now, Officer Johnson will make sure you get home safely."

I was much too numb to argue with anyone. I'd seen enough dead bodies for a lifetime in just three days. I wasn't giving up, but it was time for Plan B.

Chapter Thirteen

T urned out, Plan B involved me, unable to sleep, deciding to sneak back to George Martinez's house before the sun rose. A few reporters were set up for the five o'clock news and one squad car guarded the house out front. There was no ambulance and no Ford Fusion. At least something had gone my way.

After my nightmare-inducing view, I knew where the bedroom was. Assuming Flores couldn't walk through walls, there must be a back door. I slipped over the neighbor's fence and dashed to George's covered patio. My hands shook as I reached for the doorknob. Half of me hoped it was locked, ending this crazy trajectory I'd found myself on.

No such luck. The knob turned, and the door pushed open without a single creak.

As I passed through the modest kitchen, waves disturbed the air around me. This felt more like the buzzing from the antique store and Albert's doorstop and, currently, my townhouse.

Through the open concept living space, I honed in on the statue of the elephant in the front window. Though it wasn't actually moving, it vibrated with the energy of memories. My skin crawled as I listened for Albert's voice. I didn't have to wait long.

Don't fight it. Embrace your gift and come find me.

Albert did seek him out. George had to be cursed too. My excitement dampened as reality reminded me the only thing George was, was dead.

I straightened my shoulders and headed to the right down the hallway where his bedroom had to be.

Someone had left the lamp on beside the bed. I took a deep breath, concentrating on the in and out, trying desperately to forget the creepy smile on the dead man's face. I didn't get the smell until I came into the enclosed space. It wasn't nearly as overwhelming as in Albert's condo, but I would never again mistake the stench of human blood to that of old food. I was grateful George had been taken away, but the stains on the mattress assured me I hadn't imagined it.

To work my way up to touching the bed, my focus fell on the nightstand and the light as I tried to control my reactions. I couldn't get over how clean it was amidst a scene of such violence. The white lamp shade didn't have a drop of blood. A yellow post-it was clearly legible: *7pm Friday Tracy Gee.*

The true horror hit me and I covered my face. He'd never make that date. He'd never get up from this bed again. I was so worried about myself and finding answers, I hadn't considered the price the victims paid. I had spoken about justice, but really just wanted to learn more about myself. Seeing another savaged body of another innocent victim morphed my curiosity—and my fear—to anger.

Maybe my curse was a gift. Maybe it was time for me to use it.

I moved to the foot of the bed with my hands held behind my back. Every nerve in my body vibrated. I wondered if I looked like the statue with the emotions radiating from it. I had to know if it was the same killer. And if it was, was he targeting cursed people or did he just hate the Collector and his art?

Did that put me on the list?

I couldn't feel the killer in the room. I would've thought the act of murder would be so emotionally charged that he'd have to leave a bit of himself somewhere. Then again, I hadn't felt him in Albert's condo until I touched the victim. My only chance might be to see him through his victim's remnant. In slow casual movements, I slipped a hand out of a glove. Time to get this over with.

As soon as I touched the blood near the headboard, the room darkened, and I screamed. No, not me, George. I stopped myself from removing my hand. I sang my mom's hymn to keep my mind centered. I needed to see what George could show me without losing myself in the process. If I wallowed in the pain of the memory, I'd be no help to him or the next victim. Somehow, I knew there would be a next victim.

George screamed again at searing pain in his right arm. *Please, George, look at the murderer. Help me catch him.* Of course, I couldn't control anything George did. He was dead and this was only a memory.

The killer leaned over my—I mean, George's—body and made a slit below his left nipple. Blood gushed out, and the pain sliced through the hymn. Warmth dripped down George's sides as the same feeling spread along mine. George yanked at his restraints.

The deep voice I'd never forget spoke to his victim, "Don't worry, George. Use your gift and you will feel much better. The Collector did."

It was the same guy. Definitely the same one. I begged George to quit staring at the ceiling and look at the killer.

The killer put a hand flat on George's chest. The perfectly manicured nails were smeared with blood. He didn't wear gloves? Talk about arrogantly confident that he couldn't be caught. My toes tingled, sending waves of pleasure all the way up my body. All pain disappeared, replaced with true happiness. How could George have felt happy on top of all that agony?

George took advantage of the momentary reprieve. "Please. Tell me what you want. You haven't made any demands."

"Oh, but you *are* giving me what I want."

That was when the pieces fell into place. That wasn't George's joy. The killer's happiness was so strong, it usurped George's own pain and fear.

The murderer loved what he was doing. George's head relaxed on the pillow as the alien emotion offered him respite from the attack. He didn't even try to shield himself as anything was better than the agony of the blade.

The dim light from the lamp hit only the side of the killer's face, and all I could see was that he was white with a dark full head of hair. I didn't sneak into a crime scene to learn something I already knew. *Come on, asshole. Show yourself.*

"And that's enough." He pulled his hand from his victim's chest.

As if he'd dunked George in acid, every nerve shrieked in renewed pain.

The onslaught was so sudden, I couldn't separate my own body from the remnant. I lost my mother's singing voice as my nerves matched his level of torture. I was being drug in. I was dying. George and I melded into one. Even as my logical mind screamed it was only a memory, that it couldn't hurt me, my curse refused to separate.

As strength fled my body, gravity took over and I fell backward, disconnecting me from the impression. I rolled in remembered agony. I flexed one muscle at a time, checking for injuries I knew couldn't be there, but the pain was so real.

"What are you doing in here, Ms. Young?" Detective Flores stood in the door, a mix of confusion and anger played across his features. He grabbed the glove I'd dropped off the floor. "What were you thinking?"

His words were very loud in my ears. He had to be angry with me, at the very least, agitated, but I couldn't feel anything beyond relief that I was alive.

By the time, I came to my senses, Flores had already hauled me out the front door. "Why in God's name would you contaminate another crime scene? What are you hiding?"

It was awkward seeing Flores's face plastered with anger but being unable to feel any of it.

I had to think of something fast. The transition from pain to joy back to pain was such a huge anomaly, I had to share. "He likes it. The killer. It makes him *really* happy." *Please believe me. Please believe me.*

Flores rubbed his face, like if he touched every muscle, he'd regain his composure. "How do you know that?"

"I just do." Even I wasn't satisfied with that answer. I needed to prove it to him. I had to tell him what I couldn't tell my friends. But how?

"I'm searching for one good reason not to arrest you right now. If you didn't remind me of..." he trailed off and looked down.

I touched his hand with my ungloved one. My curse felt blown out—like hearing after a rock concert—weaker, but not broken. Heartburn mixed with muscle spasms in my legs pointed to guilt with sprinkles of fear.

I didn't know enough about him to decipher what it meant. I retrieved my glove from his grasp, like that was why I had touched him to begin with, and slipped it on. I thought of the first day I'd met Flores and sat at his desk. It was piled with cases. He must care about them, or he'd hide them away. Out of sight, out of mind.

I knew what I could do. "I can help you solve the diary case."

Flores swung around, now fully angry as my tightened gut proved. "You did look in the diary. How did you get it open without—"

"I didn't." I held up my hands, pleading with him to give me a chance. I had to give him something. Maybe it was time to come clean. "I can sense things sometimes."

Flores crossed his arms over his badge around his neck.

"That's ridiculous." Though something in the way he said the word made me believe he didn't think it was ridiculous at all.

"Let me show you. The boyfriend didn't do it." At least, I really didn't think the boyfriend did it.

He tilted his head and met my eyes again. "We were certain he did. But his alibi checks out. It's solid."

I flexed my fingers like warming up before exposing myself to more horrible things that I didn't want to see. "Take me to the scene and I will find your killer."

Chapter Fourteen

After moving Walter to the wall by the TV, farthest away from my bedroom, and covering him with all the blankets I owned, the impressions quieted to a soft murmur I could only hear within touching distance. The insulation from the remnants along with my recent nights of restlessness allowed me the best sleep I'd had all week. I was grateful Flores had insisted on a nap and shower before he took me anywhere. I tried not to be offended by the uniformed officer in front of my house. Flores wanted to believe me. But he wouldn't turn off his cop brain long enough to let it make sense. I was ready to prove it to him.

I woke up recharged and starving. Disappointment overtook my moment of excitement as my empty cabinets reminded me I hadn't had time to hit the store yet.

In the middle of my shower, my phone beeped. I toweled my face and hands dry and wrapped my hair out of the way. Flores promised to take me to the crime scene of the diary case so I could prove my claim, but hadn't set a time. No growling stomach or eye full of soap would make me miss it.

Flores: *I'm here.*

Me: *I'll be right out.*

I'd never gotten dry so fast in my life. It was weird to run out the door with wet hair and no makeup.

As I slid into the passenger seat of his dark-colored Ford Fusion, I noticed Flores's fresh suit fit him perfectly. As I pondered the inaccuracies of detectives on TV, I pulled a foot onto my lap to properly buckle the sandals I slipped on as I rushed out the door.

For some reason, he eyed me suspiciously. "You didn't have enough time to get ready? Didn't you know when I'd be here?"

My wet hair hung heavy on my back as I shook my head. "You didn't give me a time."

"But I thought..." he trailed off, but hesitated as he went to put the car in gear.

Oh, I get it. "I can't tell the future. I can just sense things."

Without a glance in my direction, he merged into early morning traffic. His doubt frustrated me, but what kind of idiot would believe this nonsense, right? I'd prove what I could do soon enough. Then he'd have to let me help with the investigation.

My confidence waned as Flores pulled into a dingy motel. What if there were no impressions? I'd never gone to a place to search for emotional baggage left behind. Well, never before this morning. Usually, I found things on accident. Would I have to touch everything in the room for the chance of encountering something useful? Maybe I should have thought this through better.

The two-story brick building with rusted railings and doors facing the parking lot sent shivers down my spine before I sensed a single thing. It didn't look brand new. There could be decades of remnants in these rooms and who knew how many random events I'd have to experience before I found anything about the teenage girl. Those specials where the reporter took a black light into the room and grossed out the audience never impressed me.

The real terrors of these rooms were the strong memories

people left behind in the "dens of sin," as my mother called them. When we'd go on family road trips—which thankfully wasn't often—my mother and I would sleep in the car rather than crash with my brothers inside. Not for the first time, I wondered if Mom had this curse. Every time I'd try to bring it up, she'd walk away and lock herself in her room. She acted that way whenever my brothers asked anything she didn't approve of, so I'd never thought of her reaction as more than denial of *my* curse.

Leaning against the second story railing, a shirtless white guy with ripped jeans and a wild beard sucked on his cigarette. His stare made me feel dirty even though I still smelled like soap. Come to think of it, it probably wasn't so safe for a woman and a little girl to sleep *outside* one of these places either. But the terrors inside the room frightened Mom way more.

Mom had a point. A part of me hoped I didn't find anything. Some of these remnants were so violent or emotionally draining, they were hard to shake off. I'd already experienced too many horrid imprints this week, and here I was voluntarily exposing myself to more. If I just turned around now, I could go back to normal life with my store and my girlfriends.

And never, ever be my authentic self.

And continue to suffer under this curse—alone.

When Flores stepped from the driver's side, the dude stomped on his cigarette and slunk behind the stairwell.

Nope. I wasn't backing out now. I *had* to find others with this curse. After a lifetime alone with this curse, I'd found two like me in less than a week. They didn't have families or significant others, but they weren't alone either. To talk to someone else about how to handle this curse without going mad myself was worth the risk of sensing more tormented experiences.

As I tied my hair up, I racked my brain for a backup plan, just in case I didn't find any evidence. "I guess there's something to be said about driving around with a cop."

"It's an unmarked car. It's not a big help." Flores scanned the parking lot. I wasn't sure if he did that consciously or out of habit.

More doors closed on the second floor, and I swear the volume of the hip-hop music that blared a moment ago grew much quieter. "It's not the car."

To his credit, Flores held up the badge around his neck. "I guess this is a dead giveaway."

"If you include the haircut and underarm holster." I sensed a bit of anxiety kind of floating in the air, just enough to make my scalp crawl like some just mentioned lice. I felt like yelling into the ether that we weren't there for them, and they could calm down. I didn't need my own emotions to feed off theirs. If this was going to work, I needed to find some sort of quiet Zen to listen for the teenager.

I walked to the door with a "14" scrawled in sharpie and a swath of police tape over the frame.

Flores reached for the handle and inserted an old-fashioned key. "Well, you chose the right door."

I pulled up the bit of police tape still stuck to the jamb. "Not really impressive work on my part."

He smiled at me. I felt the kindness in his words and some pain. This case must mean something to him. He ushered me in first and flipped the light.

I almost reached back and flipped it back off. The drab yellow light from the greasy fixture threw the room into a time warp. The sheets of the unmade full-sized bed looked bleached, but smelled like stale sex. The shabby bedspread lay on the ground, curled up like a used tissue.

Man, whoever brought her to this place spent a lot of money on their quality time. Not. Maybe I was wrong. Who else but another teenager would think this was a romantic spot to meet? Plus, it was probably all he could afford.

The carpet crunched as I circled around the comforter on the floor. I said a prayer of thanks that I didn't see any blood. I wasn't sure I could handle another mutilation scene.

As I tucked my leather gloves into a pocket, I searched for a place to start. "It's not the boyfriend," I said it out loud as much to convince myself as to tell Flores that I could help him.

His body tensed and he crossed his arms. "Family can't always be trusted when it comes to alibis."

I tentatively touched the headboard. Nothing. "When he found the diary, he left behind nothing but despair and pain. No anger or revenge lingered on the book itself. No guilt."

Unwilling to look up and see Flores staring at me like I was insane, I concentrated on the bed. Something called to me. Oh, dear God, please don't be something gross. I flipped the pillow over and put both hands on its uncovered surface. My mind slipped into the memory.

Panic. I can't breathe. He's so strong. I clawed his arms trying to get him off me. The pillow comes up a bit. I, no she—it wasn't me—took a deep breath and pleaded, "I won't tell. I promise. I love you." The soft pillow turned unrelenting as it smothered her completely.

Chapter Fifteen

I couldn't bear to experience her last moments of betrayal and confusion. With a jump backward, I rammed into the side table. I clawed at the memory of his muscled arms. I needed to separate myself, but I couldn't breathe.

A calm voice broke through the trauma, "Fauna, you're safe."

Flores's touch flowed with emotional fortitude, as warmth calmed my tense muscles. I soaked it up like a thirsty traveler in the desert. When I regained my normal breathing, I shrugged to get him to let go, which he did immediately. How did he know to do that?

He looked at me with those doe-like eyes, and my voice stuck in my throat, preventing any words from escaping. Instead, I pointed at the pillow. He shook his head and raised his eyebrows. Well, good for him, he wasn't going to risk telling me anything.

A flash of anger helped me find my voice again. "He smothered her with the pillow."

"Her cause of death was not mentioned to the press. You couldn't know that." With a step backward to lean on the dresser with a missing drawer, Flores stared at the fallen pillow like it was a ghost. Somehow, he still managed to appear in control though I could feel the turmoil he struggled with. "I'll call crime scene to come pick it up."

So, I pulled one rabbit out of a hat. Could I actually find her killer? I chickened out on full disclosure with my girlfriends, because I couldn't bear losing them. With Flores, I had nothing but possibilities. If he thought I was a loon, then I'd be no worse off than I was right now. If he believed me, I might actually find some answers to the deaths of the cursed.

"I experienced the moment of her death when I touched the pillow. That's how I know." There. I'd said it.

He did that head down-eyes up pose he seemed to favor. "So, you read minds?"

Does it look like that pillow has a mind? "No." My shoulders rolled, and my neck cracked as I tried to relieve tension and remain calm. "Sometimes, when someone experiences a life altering event, the strong emotions—positive or negative—produce enough energy to leave behind a remnant." I rubbed my forehead and paced as much as I could in the limited space. "At least, that's how I think it works. I've never explained this to anyone before."

Flores's expression hadn't changed. "You're doing fine."

A bit of hope loosened the tension. Maybe he wouldn't lock me in a padded room.

"I'm not sure I understand it myself. But I can sense the objects that hold these remnants. If I touch one, I experience the memory like it was my own. Their emotions become mine. I hear what they hear, see what they see, feel what..."

I flicked a tear from my eye. I hated feeling vulnerable. I refused to look up and see pity in Flores's eyes.

The vision gave me an idea. "Also, she clawed his arms while fighting. I bet the boyfriend's arms are clean, aren't they?"

His voice all business, Flores had his phone in his hand again. "The M.E. found samples under her fingernails, but there was no DNA match in the system." He stood up straight, his set face mirrored his now quiet soul. He must have come to some sort of decision. "Did you see the guy's face? I mean, did she see his face."

My head cocked itself at his careful phrasing and almost instant understanding. Did he believe me? It couldn't be this easy, could it? "She didn't see anything around the pillow, but she felt betrayal and said that she promised she wouldn't tell anyone." I swallowed bile that rose at the memory. "She knew her murderer."

Flores typed away on his phone, taking notes like at the other crime scenes. I didn't even know the girl, hadn't seen a single picture, but after what happened to her, I wanted to catch the guy. Badly. My arms itched and the vison of Albert's killer's scarred arms flashed to the forefront. Could they be the same guy? Surely, there hadn't been enough time to pass for such wounds to scar over since it was still an active case. Plus, the teenager wasn't stabbed. But maybe that was where the killer's scars originated. Which would mean Albert wasn't his first victim.

While reaching for the pillow to search for more clues, a tingle near the floor tickled my skin. There was another impression. I couldn't tell if it was from the teenager or not, but I wasn't going to walk away without knowing for sure. On my knees, I waved a hand under the mattress honing the location of the remnant. The buzzing in my fingers lead me to the headboard. A flash of gold from a tiny charm on a thin chain swung from a piece of the broken box springs.

I couldn't make much out, but I sensed a young woman. It had to be hers. If it wasn't, this damn place needed to be shut down for underage activity.

"What did you find? Crime Scene scoured this place."

With a folded glove, I pulled the chain free. "Well, they missed this." I floated it above my unprotected hand. The charm was a simple gold heart, fat and healthy, and heavy with love. After a nod of approval from Flores, I touched it.

My heart pounded and my stomach felt light. The charm

folded into my palm in the same way it had hers. It was definitely the same girl, in much happier times. I wish I could
preserve this memory of her and share it with her family. She
was so much in love and the joy tickled every nerve even as her
hands shook with nerves. She blinked back tears as she smiled at
the face of her love, her future.

While fighting back my own tears, I forced myself to concentrate on his face. It was definitely not a teenage boyfriend. A
middle-aged white man with sun-tanned skin smiled with a
mouth full of shiny veneers. No way those were natural. His
short, cropped, light hair and purple polo screamed teacher. I
was pretty sure there was a school mascot on the breast, but she
didn't look down long enough for me to pick it out. The man
bent over to kiss her.

I dropped the necklace onto the bed before I felt his dry lips.
A shiver climbed down my spine as my feeling of disgust fought
with her feeling of adoration. Why did young girls fall for
teachers who obviously only wanted one thing?

My face flushed as I realized Flores was staring at me expec-
tantly. "A teacher gave her this. His teeth were perfect and he
had a full head of blond hair, though it was cropped short. I
couldn't quite make out the logo on the polo, but…"

The air trembled around Flores, a sensual reflection of his
excitement. He held up a picture from his phone. "Is this the
guy?"

That horrible predatory smile took up the screen. "That's the
one."

Flores cursed under his breath, as he traded his phone for an
evidence bag and plucked the necklace off the bed.

"You don't have to curse quietly. I feel exactly the same way
right now." I re-gloved my hands and tucked them protectively
out of touching range. That was enough for one day. Even
though I'd experienced more extreme memories that were not
my own, something about catching a predator lifted my spirits. I

never considered this curse of mine to be a tool to help someone.

The entire drive home, we didn't say a word. As I reached for the car door handle, I had to know.

"A deal's a deal, right? I helped you solve that case, and you'll keep me in the loop with the Collector's."

Flores put in an address on his police device. "A deal's a deal," he said without looking up.

As he drove away into the darkening sky, I had a feeling a certain teacher was going to have a very bad day indeed.

Chapter Sixteen

The music thumped through to my core as the first couple of shots numbed my abilities. Dancing at a busy club where everyone was tipsy and feeling no pain was my favorite pastime. Usually, human touch came with physical consequences for me, but I never brought my gloves to the floor. Here, with everything spinning from alcohol, the feelings came in bursts, a specialized drug just for me. Instead of torture, I got high from the emotional whirlwind.

Plus, most of the feelings at this time of night, in this kind of place, revolved around sex. Lust dripped in the air along with the condensation from the air conditioning. After my week of murder and torment, I really needed this escape. Luckily, Amelia and Gina loved the scene as much as I did.

Amelia's short hair stuck out in purposeful spikes as her head bobbed from side to side. My bare arms brushed hers, and I didn't even cringe. My legs could barely move in the tight leather skirt that creaked when I walked—but in the club with the music blaring, a squeaky skirt was not even a blip on the radar—so I did a great deal of bouncing. My muscles welcomed the exertion.

Gina squeezed her tiny form through the crowd with our

fresh round of drinks. Her smooth, dark hair shimmered with glitter which refracted the rotating lights. She always said it would break her Vietnamese mother's heart if she dyed her hair. So, she chose washable alternatives, glitter being her favorite. I thought it had more to do with all that left-over glitter from class. I hadn't been to her house since she started teaching, but I bet the carpet sparkled with it.

We clinked the glasses together and took a generous sip. The cranberry and Malibu blend tasted sweet and sour and refreshing, like sparkling water on the tongue. Though my hangover in the morning would remind me that it wasn't water, right now, I didn't care.

As if the addition of booze to our circle of friendship was an invitation, a smoking hot Hispanic man smiled at me like a wolf drooling over a steak. I welcomed the attention. That was what I needed. I swayed my hips to the reggae-hip-hop blend the DJ had chosen. Mr. Wolf stepped my way so smoothly it felt choreographed. Gina and Amelia found themselves similarly engaged and I let them go to concentrate on my chosen target.

That was the thing about dancing. I could tell what a man would be like in bed by the way he moved me around the floor. Mr. Wolf pulled me close forcefully, but not violently. Oh yeah. I was on board. His hips forced mine to rotate with him. With his desire strong enough to penetrate my drunken haze, I knew he was as into me as much as I was into him. His emotions got me high, as my lust and his combined and heightened my enthusiasm.

I stood on my tiptoes to yell into his ear. "Fauna." There was something so intimate about screaming your name into a stranger's ear and no one else being able to hear you.

"Chipped girl?"

I jumped back at the voice that was somewhat familiar. My neck burned, reflecting Mr. Wolf's surprise at the interruption. To my left, the man who had been dancing with Amelia had turned his attention to me. His blue eyes glowed through the dim light of the club as if they had a light source all their own.

It was the guy that picked up the stolen computer. "Tucker?"

The smile that put all the right creases in the right places made my heart thump my ribs much harder than the bass from the speakers. "You remembered. But I don't know your name?"

He had to lean down close so I could hear him. Chills ran down my spine as the smell of him—leather and vanilla with a background of antiseptic—mixed with his simple happiness. I swooned from more than the rum.

I managed to pull myself together and shouted back into his ear. "Fauna."

From over his shoulder, Amelia tilted her head and her hips in opposite directions.

I mouthed, "Mine," then gestured with a slight nod behind me to the hot Hispanic man, "yours."

With a shrug, she danced behind us and took my spot in the arms of Mr. Wolf. He didn't even look back at me, as his gaze was captured by Amelia's cleavage. She preferred the smoldering hot kind of guy anyway. I just did her a favor.

As the song changed to a more frantic tune, Tucker scratched the back of his neck and watched with an almost panicked expression at the gyrating bodies around him. I took his hands, the nervousness swimming within him crawled along my scalp.

This was obviously not his scene. "I haven't seen you here before."

"What was the first clue? My stiff hips or my lost boy look." He tried to dance like the fluid man in leather pants next to us.

I couldn't remember laughing so hard at a club that didn't feature a comedian. "So why tonight?"

He gestured to a couple rowdy men near the stage trying to get the DJ to change the song. "It's one of the resident's bachelor party. I tried to get the late shift to avoid it, but..." He waved his hands around his head like a drunk sorority girl.

I had to help the boy out. "Relax. It's not that hard."

My hands found his hips and pulled him against mine. As I swayed, his rhythm improved greatly. His nervousness faded, and his cheeks flushed. His fingertips brushed hair out of my face, and his desire enhanced my own. My grin had to engulf my face as I felt that itch morph into a throbbing in my lady bits. He wanted me as badly as I wanted him. All of the talking sobered me up too much, I needed another drink to keep everything dulled enough to stay in control.

On my tiptoes to get my voice as close to his ear as possible, I pressed my body against his, feeling his excitement. He might not be a regular member of the club scene, but he was certainly having a good time now. "Want another drink?"

After swallowing so dramatically, I felt it in *my* chest, Tucker nodded emphatically.

Unwilling to peel myself away from his warm body, I nevertheless forced myself to pull away to find my girlfriends. "There's one more thing I need to do."

Spotting the two a couple feet away with their perspective prospects, I navigated the crowd to get close enough to grab Amelia's and Gina's hands. I kissed the tops, as was our preassigned signal for the end of our evening as a trio and the beginning of my night as a duo.

Gina pouted, like one of her students. "But we just got here."

"Have fun!" Amelia spun Mr. Wolf around.

After adjusting my top to make sure the girls looked perfect, I turned around to find Tucker so close, my swirling hair hit him.

My heart stopped as my arms crossed protectively. His blue eyes shadowed from the lights of the stage reminded me of Albert's last memory, of the psychic's last view. My legs froze in place or I swear I would have run away screaming. All of the heavy petting and sexy innuendo faded to cold fear.

He pushed sweat from his forehead, seemingly oblivious to my change in demeanor. "Are you ready for that drink now?"

His forearms glimmered as he motioned toward the bar.

Unmarred, perfect—though pale—skin reflected the neon lights. It was my turn to swallow heavily. He wasn't the guy. Thank God, because I had to see the naked chest attached to those strong arms. Now more than ever. This whole murder investigation was really getting to me. Suspecting every blue-eyed white guy I met would lead to a world of paranoia. Plus, Tucker was blond, and the killer had dark hair.

I twisted my fingers into Tucker's and led him away from the dance floor. He followed as I wove between the rest of the clubbers, his hand never leaving mine. I was impressed. Sometimes, the man I chose refused to let me lead at all. This was going to be a good night.

I stumbled a bit. Tucker caught me with an easy confidence. I had never taken home the same man twice. Sex was fun. Relationships were painful. I admit, it was a bit weird considering a man I'd met at work. As large as Houston seemed from the outside, it felt much smaller when I continuously ran into the same people over and over again.

Even though I was certain he was not the nightmare that attacked Albert and George, it didn't mean he wasn't some other sort of malcontent. Of all people, I knew full well that the inside didn't always match the outside. Before I went home with anyone—even a man who stopped by after work to do a favor for his sister—I needed to safety check first. A woman could never be too careful.

That was something men didn't seem to understand. It wasn't that women didn't want sex. My soaking wet panties were indication enough. Women hesitated to go home with a guy, because they were afraid he would hurt them. That was one thing I could always discover—my chosen partner's intentions. I never failed to check before I left with one.

I waved the bartender over. "One more shot, Jim. For me and Tucker here. Then close me out."

Jim gave me a thumbs up and waggled his thin eyebrows at my chosen. I winked at the bartender. His arm muscles flexed as he rubbed cut limes on two shot glasses. He salted the tops and attached the citrus to the sides. After pouring generous portions of Milagro in each, he slid them along the bar to Tucker and me. If Jim wasn't gay, I would have shown him a good time already. As it was, I had to settle for tipping generously, which I did.

Tucker cocked his head at me.

Oh no, he better not be judging me now, just when he was about to see it all. "What?"

Tucker's grin melted my anger like it had yesterday. "You look much more comfortable here than you did in your own store."

Interesting. He actually took the time to register my mood yesterday. Most guys barely note more than surprise that a woman runs a computer store. I held up my shot to clink with Tucker. "Welp. A bit of magical elixir and a hot guy on her arm tends to relax a girl."

His face flushed. "Hot, am I?"

With my whole body pressed against his, I lifted my glass to my lips. He stopped my wrist and bent down and licked the salt off my glass. I laughed as his playful mood tickled my toes. It made me forget all the horrible things I'd seen in the past couple of days. He used my hand as a handle and leaned down to dump the shot down his throat, then sucked on the lime for an obscene amount of time.

My turn to put on a show. I hiked my skirt up enough to hop onto a barstool. I took his wrist as he had mine and brought it slowly to my lips. Electricity sparked into my fingers from his heightened excitement. The feelings of his lust and my own intermingled created a much more intoxicating effect than the alcohol. My tongue lashed out and rimmed the glass of its salt. Taking the shot from his slack hand, I downed the tequila. My chest thrust out as the burn barreled down my throat. I moaned as I sucked the juice out of the lime, soothing the heat of the alcohol.

Tucker's muscles radiated heat as he braced his weight on the bar top on either side of me. "I don't know what it is about you, Fauna, but I'm ready to get out of this bar."

I wrapped my ankles around the back of his knees and pulled him closer. "I feel it too."

Now for the final test. As he pressed his lips to mine, his muscled chest rippled against my breast. My tongue welcomed his attention as the heat of tequila and the sour lime twisted together in both of our mouths. My nipples were on fire. No amount of tequila would dull this strong of a feeling. For a moment, the sensations swallowed me whole, and I almost forgot I was supposed to get a deep reading.

With my hands woven behind his neck, I curved my stomach up to meet his and dropped what little barriers I had up. Though tempered by the alcohol I'd consumed, his emotional being opened up to me. Right on top was lust, hot and needy. Underneath was desire, not of sex, but to please. It took me forever to identify that one; I'd not experienced it as often as I would have hoped. This was going to be an incredible night, just what I needed. But I needed to go deeper.

As I breathed through my nose, because my mouth was completely locked down, I concentrated on Tucker, blocking out the music and the emotions in the air and my own needs. Within him, I felt no anger, no violence, a little self-doubt—which surprised me coming from this hunk. Oh, heartache; he needed a pick-me-up too. Something had happened, whether a breakup or a job loss or a death in the family, I couldn't tell. Something harsh enough to leave a fresh scar. I took one more moment to make sure there was nothing deeper, angrier.

Sometimes, I wished I could read minds. There would be so much less interpretation. But this wasn't my first rodeo, and I'd sensed all of these conditions before, though not in exactly the same way. No one's inner self was ever identical to anyone else's. Yet, I made my living for a few years with these deep reads. I was damn good at it.

After a thorough investigation that I might have let linger a bit longer than normal due to his expert kissing, I was confident Tucker had no ill-will toward me. And if I learned anything, he needed this as much as I did.

I jumped as amusement from a third party intruded my open senses.

Jim patted me on the shoulder. "Your Uber is here."

My trusty bartender thought I was funny. Who needed an Alfred when I had a Jim? "Thanks!"

Tucker pushed back from the bar and helped me off the stool. "When did you order an Uber?"

"Magic. Now what's your address? It's time to scale this party down to naked." My cheeks flushed at my idiocy. I had no idea what I was saying. I wanted to get back to lust and away from conversation.

I strutted toward the door with as much grace as my drunk ass could handle. Looking over my shoulder, I cocked my head at Tucker. He practically sprinted to my side. Maybe I would give him my number.

Chapter Seventeen

Tucker proved to be everything I had imagined. Even his gentle snoring in his bed—that we thoroughly destroyed—was appealing. My curse was numb with the overuse as a few other body parts throbbed with the memory. I considered waking him and having one more go before I left.

I stopped myself though, because that would be breaking my cardinal rule: no relationships, just hook ups. My finger traced his back muscles to his thick shoulder blade. What the heck. I wasn't Catholic. Screw the cardinal rule.

Oh boy, these conversations I had with myself cracked me up. I couldn't even get along with my own thoughts. How the hell was I going to make a relationship work? Plus, I came here fair and square with no expectations.

The streetlight from outside highlighted the clean condo with fresh-pressed scrubs hanging in the closet. At least, Tucker wasn't a slob. I'd been to some awful places to feed my appetite, but this one was pretty nice. My aching muscles encouraged me to snuggle closer and fall asleep. A groan escaped my lips as reason attempted to win over the alcohol haze. I'd never stayed until morning. I wouldn't even know how to handle myself in the daylight.

Sober.

After rolling out of bed as quietly as I could manage, I played my favorite post-sex game: Where were my clothes? My shirt was easy. It was always easy because it was always right by the door. Every time. As I scoured his apartment to reassemble my outfit, I felt amazing, except for the lost-in-the-desert-sized thirst. I opened his fridge but didn't see any water. A beer would have to do. I twisted the top off and downed it.

By the time I squeezed back into my impossible leather skirt, it was just past 1 a.m.

Having no idea where I was, I took another beer from the fridge and snuck out the door. By the time I hit the street, the second beer was almost gone. I remembered getting there, but most of the time, my face was stuck in Tucker's and I didn't actually pay attention to the streets or the area of town I ended up in. I squinted at the CVS across the street and then saw my favorite Mexican restaurant.

Midtown. Oh, good. I knew exactly where I was.

As I fumbled for my phone to summon a ride, realization of what else I was next to hit me.

My mood dropped, as did the bottle I'd been holding.

"Shit!" I yelled as the dregs in the bottle splashed on my legs and glass sprinkled the sidewalk where normal, not-drunk-on-a-weekday people would walk tomorrow.

I tried to restore my mood and block the bloody scene from Sunday, the event that changed my life. Maybe I should have stayed in bed with that scrumptious Tucker. I yanked my fingers through my hair, like the strands were in my face blurring my vision, not the copious amounts of alcohol I'd consumed. The blue building a couple blocks down, however, was in perfect focus.

The alcohol probably didn't help, but I swung from shock to pure anger. How dare he do this to me! How dare he ruin what little peace I had! My life might have been lonely before, but it was quiet and safe. And now I didn't know what the hell was going on.

How many cursed were there? Why couldn't Albert Johnson, the artist, the Collector, just post a video on YouTube or go on a morning talk show or put an ad on Craigslist? Why did he have to assault me emotionally with that damn statue out of nowhere? How did he put this desperate need into me to find out the truth?

Well, you know what? Fuck him.

I stomped down the road to the building. The door that had been unlocked before through the garden was still unlocked. This was a terribly unsafe building. They needed to get that fixed. The whole way up the elevator, I adjusted my tiny purse strap over my shoulder. Its attempts at escape made me second guess my breaking into his apartment. Plus, what were the odds that the red door would be unlocked this time? As the elevator doors closed behind me, I remembered the smell.

The body was hauled out by the police. Surely, it wouldn't smell anymore, right? A glance down the hallway showed my vomit had been cleaned up. Maybe his condo wouldn't be so bad.

Dammit. Why was this so hard? I needed answers, and they were in the apartment. If this psycho was targeting people like me, I could be next.

Son of a bitch. Maybe I drank too much. Who would know about my curse anyway? Which begged the question, how did the killer know about anyone's?

The door didn't budge. That would have been too easy. I leaned against the wood and felt the top of the door jamb. That was where all the keys were in the movies. My fingers brushed a sticky substance of unknown origin that I tried not to think about, but no cold metal key. I slid down the door and dropped my head into my hands.

This was dumb anyway. I pulled out my phone to call an Uber like I should have as soon as I hit the street. My fingers had trouble following the directions of my alcohol-addled mind. The fluorescent hallway lights didn't help. There was something intolerable about being drunk when it was bright. Fumbling with my phone, I accidentally hit the YouTube app popping up the DIY eyeliner video I watched while getting ready for this evening.

A new idea popped into my head. I rolled onto my knees and scrutinized the lock. It looked like a simple bolt with the name etched into the top. I typed in "how to pick a deadbolt" and the specific brand. Bam! What did we ever do without the internet? With a couple hairpins retrieved from my perfectly coifed hair— well, it was before Tucker anyway—I got to work.

By the time, I finally got the lock to click open, my forehead was slick with sweat and my fingers ached from constantly twisting and poking with the bent hairpins. That damn tutorial made it look a lot easier than it was. I pushed the red door open and fell flat on my face. My legs had gone completely numb.

Still on the floor, I took a whiff of the air before I went any further. I could still smell the sour sweet decomposition, but it floated underneath the surface instead of slamming me in the face. While I wondered how they were ever going to rent out this condo again, I managed to find my feet.

The impressions on the large shelf at the entrance vibrated, but not insistently like the first time. I wasn't going to run away this time. I was going to use them for answers. Now where to start? Albert chose to call himself the Collector, right? There had to be some sort of pattern to the disparate items. Why did he choose these? My hand hovered over a huge silver belt buckle. My stomach lurched.

Before I searched for clues, I needed another drink. My brain still swam in alcohol, but concentrating on the lock had forced a bit of sobriety to the forefront. I wasn't ready to think straight. I might decide to do the right thing and go home and sleep it off when I really needed answers.

Reluctant to go into the kitchen, I concentrated on his desk.

There had to be liquor here somewhere. A large black and white office calendar sat on the desk, a big "X" marked in the corner of each Friday night along with notes on upcoming shows. The middle drawer had nothing but a stapler and some pencils.

"Those marks better not be AA meetings." The top side drawer had miscellaneous office supplies and a few napkins with sketches on them. "No clubs on the napkins? Come on, Albert. I can't imagine you had to live with everyone else's feelings and didn't drink."

Out of desperation, I went into the kitchen. The blood had been cleaned up, but stains still marred the floor. I walked around the spot where I found him. The flashback already rolled across my mind. I didn't need the added assault of the actual remnant.

The fridge contained an old carton of milk and some moldy vegetables. "Seriously, Albert? No beer. Were you some sort of health nut?"

A quick check in the cabinet over the stove produced nothing. Under the sink was only cleaning supplies. "You really do go to AA meetings every Friday, don't you?"

I leaned on the sink. Before I realized what I'd touched, someone else's memory of pure joy rushed through my limbs. With my senses numbed, I easily separated my own experience, but it didn't make it any less disturbing. He was happy. He'd found it. After all this time, he knew.

Chapter Eighteen

I tore my hands away. My lungs heaved as adrenaline incited every nerve.

That was Albert's killer. Unless I was totally off my mark, George Martinez's too.

How could the sadistic bastard be so ecstatically happy after brutally murdering another human being? It was exactly what he felt—and made George reflect—at the psychic's house. What was going on here? I swallowed my anger and used it to fuel my determination. My artificially sobered brain watched the emotional vibrations disturb the air from the collection of impressions near the door.

It was time to get down to business.

Before the cluttered shelves, I pressed my hands to my hips and cracked my neck. It was the best tough bitch pose I could manage. The answers had to be on these damn impressions, and I was going to find it. But first, I had to center myself. I'd never searched for an object on purpose before the hotel this afternoon with Flores. If I was going to survive this attempt, if I was going to use this curse to help find a killer, I had to learn to reliably separate myself from the experiences of the people who left the remnants.

Studying the myriad pieces, I wasn't sure where to start. Trophies sat next to rusty tools on the same shelf with toys and gaudy jewelry. Some of the items had tags with numbers, while others had no discernible markings. I couldn't make heads or tails of the mess.

Enough procrastinating. I needed to choose an impression and touch it.

My hands curled into fists as I reached toward a teddy bear. My mom's favorite hymn floated in the background as I held the object just below its arms. Inside the memory, I squeezed the bear to my nightgown, like a protective barrier.

No, I had to stop thinking like that. I was not wearing a nightgown. This memory was not mine. Breathe.

The girl—I was sure it was a girl—shook, as her nervousness shot adrenaline through her muscles. She shifted on her bed under the covers, like she couldn't get comfortable. The foot of the mattress compressed and she looked up at a white man in his mid-thirties in a T-shirt and sports shorts.

"I won't hurt you, sweetheart," he said, as he tossed the cap from his head onto the side table. He pulled his bangs up from their flattened position with his right hand.

I dropped the teddy bear. Why would Albert keep that? It should be burned. Kicking the horrible remnant aside, I forcibly cleared my mind of the disgust I felt. I had to try the next one. I avoided a child-sized skate. A fountain pen fit nicely in my palm.

Fear flowed from this one. My—his—hand holding the expensive pen had almost opaque skin folded among deep purple veins. He knew he was dying, and his helplessness overshadowed a bitter sadness. He tried to resist, but her hand over his was too strong.

A middle-aged white woman held the clipboard with his written will. "Don't worry, Dad. I'll make sure your legacy continues without the influence of those illegitimate nightmares. I am your true daughter and always will be."

His throat contracted around something lodged within that

prevented him from speaking. Based on the wheezing sounds in the background, he was probably intubated. Though his muscles no longer obeyed, his mind was sharp and full of betrayal.

I pushed the pen aside letting the remnant fade. I wondered if the fake will held up in court.

The next item was a funny looking totem pole. It reminded me of that horrible episode of the Brady Bunch when they went on vacation in Hawaii. Well, let's see what curse this one held.

Its carved surface bit into the palm of the impression-leaver. Boys piled on top of him in some field in the middle of the night. His chest ached as he tried to pull in air. He couldn't pull in enough to yell at them to get off as he sunk into the mud.

The guys crushing him chanted Greek letters. The bitter smell of hops floated in the air like a brewery had exploded. The man under all the testosterone feebly smacked the nearest cheek with the totem.

Their eyes met and the one above freaked out. "Get off! Quick! There's something wrong." Though right next to the totem holder's head, the voice sounded like it came from far away.

As sweet, fresh air rushed into his lungs, a tight pain gripped his chest. As someone flipped him over, the totem holder scratched at his chest, unable to breathe even after the pile-on dissipated.

I pushed the totem aside and rested my forehead on the bookshelf, my hand massaging the pain in my own chest. What kind of sick collection was this? What kind of man was Albert Johnson that he chose to surround himself with so many visceral memories of horrible things happening to real people? If I was going to collect emotional remnants, I'd want ones like that charm where the girl was so much in love. Those are the things we need to hold on to, not the treacherous things we do to each other.

A bowling trophy stood tall by my hand. This one had to be a happy memory. Every aspect of life was not misery. Pretending to have more hope than I felt, I wrapped my hand around the trophy's bright green column. Fury added force to every blow as the man bludgeoned another with the base of the trophy.

"Enough!" I yelled, and threw the trophy across the living room. It smashed into the wall with a satisfying crunch. Pieces scattered across the floor. "You too." I accused the fountain pen and threw it across the room.

I'd had it. I wasn't learning anything, just torturing myself. I picked up one piece after another and flung it across the room. The beginning of an emotion would hit—every time an unpleasant one—then I'd add it to the flying debris. I don't know what I thought I'd find, but I was stupidly naive for thinking I could solve such a mystery.

A hammer swung through the air and went right through the wall, ripping a huge swath of wallpaper. Oh shit, I'd done it now.

With my hands on my knees to catch my breath from the all-out temper tantrum, I noticed that the hammer flew through the wall, but I didn't remember hearing it break anything. After scooting around the litter on the floor, I knelt on the couch to inspect the damage. There was nothing solid behind the peeling patch of wallpaper, just a rough rectangle sawed into the drywall. Inside, the light from my phone highlighted a brown leather ledger, like the one I used to keep the books at work. With my hand shaking, too exhausted to fight anymore impressions, I reached in and touched the cover.

Relief relaxed my tension. I felt nothing. It was clean.

I dropped onto a cushion, cross-legged, and opened the book. Columns and columns of numbers filled page after page. More mysteries on top of more mysteries. Where were the answers? What could all of these numbers mean? There must be a guide somewhere. I scoured the hole in the wall. There wasn't anything else in there.

"Ms. Young?"

I fell right off the couch and face planted. I rolled over, and stared up at a uniformed policeman, the same one who found me Sunday night in much the same compromising position.

"Officer Pradock, I need to talk to Detective Flores, right away." I pointed at the ledger, then the torn wallpaper. "I found this in there. It has to be a clue."

He reported to his radio that he was arresting an intruder and the address. As he helped me to my feet, I really wished I had my gloves and maybe a bit more skin covered. His emotional state reflected concern and annoyance in equal parts. And though minor on the scale of emotional reactions, after the night I'd had, it was too much for me to handle. The onslaught of mental images and experiences and the excessive drinking without water hit me with a swirl of nausea, and I blacked out.

Chapter Nineteen

My body shivered with cold as I rolled awake. Where was all the light coming from? My room was never this bright. With rapid blinking to mitigate the painful glow, I managed to pry one eye open, only to have a stabbing pain in my brain make me close it again. Usually a slight headache, easily dealt with by a couple ibuprofen, was the only sign of excessive alcohol use. This was the worst hangover I'd ever had.

What did I do last night? Warmth traveled down my spine at the memory of Tucker. Then the afterward came back in a sweep of anger and tormented memories. My wrist ached from throwing those remnants during my temper tantrum at Albert's condo. It was probably a good thing that Officer Pradock—*Oh shit.*

I sat up in one motion. My hands gripped the base of the cot to keep me upright as the room continued to spin. Instead of my dark, cozy bedroom, bars surrounded me in a sparse room with only the thin, elevated mattress I sat on and a dingy toilet.

Jail. How the heck did I end up in jail? My memory was so foggy I didn't remember leaving Albert's.

On either side of me were two more empty cells. I rubbed the chill from my arms. The skin-to-skin contact threw me for a loop. Where were my gloves? I was in a police station with heaven knows what kind of riff raff and emotional baggage, and I had no protection. My short leather skirt and skimpy top did little to protect the rest of my body. When my elbow had slightly brushed that journal, I was inundated with unwanted images and emotions. A place like this might have all kinds of remnants. I didn't think my brain could take much more torment.

I had to get out of here. "Hey! Who's watching this place? No one read me my rights. You can't hold me."

Now I understood how the big cats at the zoo felt as I mirrored their pacing. I wasn't going to rub on the bars though. No obvious impressions vibrated on the metal, but that didn't mean one wouldn't pop up as soon as I touched it.

"Don't I get a phone call or something?" My own voice made my head throb more. I ignored the pain for the chance at freedom. "What time is it? Is Detective Flores in yet?"

My arms waved like a stranded driver at a camera buzzing in the corner. "Is anyone paying attention? I could really use a drink." My mouth was as dry as parchment from a desert cave. Though my burps tasted like stale beer. "Of water. I mean a drink of water."

A door opened with an echoed bang at the end of the hallway, followed by the rhythmic clack of men's dress shoes on the concrete floor. A uniformed officer accompanied Detective Collins to my cell. That was not who I hoped would come to my rescue. He obviously didn't care for me much.

Collins munched on a kolache and sipped a steaming cup of coffee. Shit. Did that mean it was morning? How long had I been out? I was supposed to work today. I had to call Jeff to cover me. I'd have had no trouble asking if Flores had walked through that door. Collins intimidated me like my older brother always had.

With my arms crossed over my chest, I tried to sound contrite. "Can I make a phone call?"

The uniformed officer swung a set of keys in his hand as if he was just there to practice.

Collins brushed a crumb from his jacket. "I haven't decided."

My fists clenched against my ribs. "I have to make sure my store is covered."

The older detective looked bored. "You should have thought of that before you broke into a crime scene—again. I'm ready to charge you."

A long sip of the warm coffee looked like the nectar of the gods to me. This torture would totally work on me. Too bad I didn't have anything to confess.

He continued his bad cop routine, an act I completely believed. "For some reason, Flores thinks you have something to offer."

At some secret cue from Collins, the officer with the keys unlocked my cell. Collins moved toward the door he'd entered from, and I didn't see any choice but to follow. He led me down a hallway to Flores standing in front of a door. I would have cried in relief if I hadn't been so dehydrated.

A bit more of the evening came back and my arms dropped. "Did you get the ledger?" I asked Flores.

"You mean the ledger from the condo that you broke into and trashed. The same condo that is an active crime scene. The one that you contaminated so egregiously that we don't know that any evidence found there will be allowed into court at all. Is that what you were referring to?"

My arms crossed back over my chest, but this time in supplication. "I might have been drinking." Like that was any sort of excuse.

"Come with me." Flores nodded at the officer, who unlocked the door.

On a small table was a plate of kolaches and two bottles of water. Off to the side was my purse, cell phone, and a set of gloves I knew I didn't have on me last night. Flores must have provided the pair.

I turned as he started to close the door. "You believe me."

His expression softened. "Let's just say, I think you need to see this."

My head titled in curiosity, but I decided to try listening. He closed the door behind him and I dived for a water bottle. The entire thing was almost drained before I realized there was someone sitting at the table on the other side of the two-way mirror. He looked familiar to me, but I couldn't quite place him.

Collins had finished his kolache and reached for another. "You should keep it down. These rooms aren't soundproof. It wasn't in the budget."

While I nibbled on fresh bread wrapped around cheese and sausage—it had to be the most delicious thing I'd ever eaten— Flores entered the adjoining interrogation room and sat down with his back to the mirror.

His voice came through a speaker in the wall, "We know you were with Cindy on the night of her murder."

Cindy? Who was that? What did she have to do with the Albert Johnson case?

The guy crossed his arms and leaned back in his chair. I couldn't sense his emotions from here, but his fingers tapping on his elbows belied his show of confidence. He was nervous. "I was, along with every other girl on the team."

I gasped and almost choked on a piece of sausage. Holy shit. That was the guy who murdered the diary girl. He gave her the necklace, and he couldn't risk her telling his wife. He was her coach?

Flores stood and paced to the side of the table. "We know more than you think we do." He placed an evidence bag with the necklace from the motel in front of the coach. "We're running your fingerprints through the crime scene evidence. It's only a matter of time before we have concrete proof. You can either tell us what happened now, or you can take your chances with the jury."

The suspect's face flushed pink as he rubbed his hands through his hair as if the correct response was hidden in the strands somewhere. "Look. I was sleeping with her, okay? It was wrong. I know that. She just kept coming on to me at every practice. I was weak. But I didn't kill her."

Flores looked at the mirror—at me. "Cindy said she wouldn't tell anyone. She said no one would ever know."

"How could you...?" The coach dropped his hands and stared with his mouth open.

Leaning toward his suspect, Flores's voice rose in anger. "And you still held that pillow over Cindy's face while she fought and scratched and screamed." He grabbed the coach's arm and yanked up his right sleeve. The skin was shredded with scratch marks.

The coach lost any semblance of control and collapsed on the table, bawling.

I froze at those familiar marks. It looked just like Albert's killer, except those were fresh. He really had murdered someone before Albert. The kolache fell from my hand as I lost my appetite at the implication.

Flores slid a notepad and a pen to the coach and told him to start writing.

Collins whistled. "He's smooth, isn't he?" He studied me with a clenched jaw. "I wonder why Flores wanted you in here."

His judgement made me feel vulnerable. I shrugged as I slipped the gloves over my exposed hands.

Flores opened the door and waved at me from the hallway. "Come on. I'll take you home." He tossed the evidence bag to Collins. "Will you finish this for me?"

Collins saluted with his coffee cup. "Whatever you say, boss."

Waves of accomplishment flowed around Flores and swelled in my chest. The tickling in my toes and fingertips helped squash the uneasiness of my revelation. "So, you got him. That was fast."

"Thanks to you."

I swallowed a bit heavier than normal due to the lump in my throat. "Does that mean you'll keep me informed of the Albert Johnson case?" I was sure I sounded desperate, because I was.

Flores nodded. "A deal's a deal."

If I was officially on the case, then I had to tell about the scars. "His arms. Those were defensive wounds, right?"

He picked up keys and his phone from his desk. "They were."

"Remember the scars I said I saw on Albert's killer's arms?"

Flores looked at me from the corner of his eye as he led me to the parking lot. "A glimpse we still need to talk about. I'd like to know how you saw anything of the killer at all."

The sun hit me from an angle as we left the building, but heat already radiated from the cement. It was going to be a scorcher today. I needed more water.

"I'll tell you everything, now that you believe me." He really did. I was full of more doubt than he was. *I* couldn't believe that this professional questioner and presumer of guilt thought I had this curse, and I wasn't just crazy or something. Maybe I should have told Gina and Amelia years ago. If Flores thought I was telling the truth, why wouldn't they? "First, I think the scars were defensive wounds, but old ones. They looked just like the coach's arms."

"Interesting." Flores beeped his car unlocked as he retrieved his phone to take more notes.

Which reminded me that Chipped should be opened soon. In my purse, my phone was as helpful as a brick. "Can I borrow your phone right quick? My battery is dead."

After I made sure Jeff had Chipped covered, I climbed into the passenger seat. "So, what's next?"

"I take you home. I have a ton of paperwork and you," his cheek twitched, "need a bath."

"What? I don't..." One whiff under my armpit made me

grateful I'd finished that last bite first. Some combination of sweat and sex and stress resulted in a revolting odor. "Okay, you win. A serious scrubbing is in order."

As we exited the parking lot, he added, "Oh, and if you ever break into a crime scene again, you'll spend a lot more time behind those bars."

Chapter Twenty

My still-damp hair smelled like vanilla as I woke up in my own bed this time. I wasn't usually a day sleeper, but damn that rest felt good. My phone laid on my nightstand, but I'd forgotten to plug it in. With a kick of the sheets, I rolled out of bed to get the plug from the kitchen.

I didn't know what I was supposed to be doing. Flores said he'd let me in, but what did that mean exactly?

A loud banging shook my door. A flash of glee from the brutal killer filled my mind and terrified me. What if he'd found me? Never one to carry a firearm, I might need to reconsider my stance.

"Fauna! Are you in there?" Amelia's voice—angry but safe— shouted from the other side. The jingle of keys added to her frustrated tone.

A huge smile of relief creased my face as I unlatched the door and swung it open. Her keys still stuck in the lock, Amelia stormed in like a hurricane and grabbed me by both of my shoulders. I shuddered as her fear clenched through my muscles. As she inspected me, her fear morphed to fury. The pit of my stomach cramped. Based on her facial expressions, the tension of my muscles and my gut might have intensified and knocked me on my butt if she hadn't released me. Amelia normally didn't touch me at all. I was super grateful for that now, because, boy, did she exude really strong emotions when she was upset.

"You never called. I've been blowing up your phone and you never answered or called me back." Her eyes bore into mine as she blinked a tear from her eye.

Sudden guilt of my own drowned out Amelia's fear. I held up my phone. "It's dead. I forgot to plug it in." And I broke into a crime scene and spent the night in a jail cell.

She blinked at me, her cheeks flushing bright red.

I wished I could take the pain from her, not just share it. "I'm sorry, Amelia. Everything was so crazy last night—"

"No, no, that's not good enough." She pushed me away and flopped down on my couch.

I pulled her keys from the lock and shut the door, as I tried to decide how much I could tell her. Flores believed me. Surely my oldest friends would too. After all, a full confession would clear up some of my quirks. Yet, I couldn't tell Amelia without Gina. It was definitely a conversation to be had once.

Instead, I leaned against the wooden frame, and waited for my deserved lecture.

After flipping tears from her cheeks with jerky swipes, Amelia glared at me. "You know, this isn't slut shaming. Both Gina and I could care less who you go home with. It's about safety. The deal is you text us when you get home so we know we don't have to start searching the hospitals. Which reminds me, *I* have to text Gina that you're alive."

It was time to get them together and make a full confession. No distractions this time. "Tell Gina I'm cooking dinner tonight."

Amelia shook her head as she typed on her phone. "Not good enough."

My shoulders sagged, as my hands flipped my phone front to back to front in a concentric pattern.

"Gina wants the full Fauna gourmet meal." Her upper lip

curved up at one corner. "And I demand that amazing dark chocolate soufflé you made for Easter."

Relief relaxed my muscles. They really were the best friends a girl could have. "Deal."

Amelia bounced up from the couch and pointed at Walter hidden by blankets next to the TV. "Is that the $3000 statue?"

"Yep."

She obviously wanted more. "Why did you spend all that money on this thing, just to hide it?"

The layers of cloth were the only reason I could stand it being in the condo at all. Until I found a better solution, that was how it was going to stay. She'd know exactly why at dinner.

Instead of a real answer, I offered, "The whims of a crazy woman."

Amelia cocked her head, clearly not satisfied. "I'll let that one slip for now. I've done enough mothering for one day, and I need to get back to work."

With my door half open, she pointed her phone at me. "You better pick up when I call."

I held up the cord from the kitchen counter with dramatic flair and plugged my phone in. "Deal."

That evening, the townhouse smelled like garlic, cream, and fresh bread from the fettuccini alfredo and homemade baguettes the three of us had devoured. Gina and Amelia filled the dishwasher as I packed up the plastic containers with leftovers.

"It was amazing, Fauna." Gina giggled as I shoved it all in the fridge. "You don't have to cook for an army every time though. We're going to have to start inviting more people."

"Oh no, we don't," argued Amelia. "Those leftovers are my lunch for the next week."

The distinct smell of chocolate wafted from the oven. "The

soufflé tells me it's done." Not quite as high as I wanted it, though the cake still blossomed above the pan in a healthy pouf.

Amelia leaned on the counter focused on the oven. "I don't know how you know it's done without a timer."

I hadn't said a thing yet about my curse. This could be the best lead in. "Sometimes, I can sense things." With a towel stretched between my hands, I pulled the dessert from the oven, careful not to splash the hot water from the roasting pan.

Her ponytail bouncing with energy, Gina grabbed three small plates from the cabinet. "I totally get that. I always know when one of my students has to use the bathroom. Experience can open up different clues."

Amelia rolled her eyes. "Sure, like I can tell when Bob is going to take credit for my work. Oh wait, that's always, so it doesn't count."

Digging the serving spoon into the steaming soufflé, I dolloped a generous portion onto each plate. I wanted to confess, but my nerves were getting the better of me with Amelia's sarcasm going strong tonight. What if she didn't take me seriously?

I had to try. "No, I mean I can actually sense like emotions and stuff from people and sometimes objects."

Amelia blinked at me, a spoon halfway to her mouth.

Gina, however, didn't seem to hear me. She grabbed her plate and spoon and moved to the living room. "Hey, can we watch the end of the Bachelor? I have it recording at home, but I won't have the energy to watch tonight. If Margie from yoga class spoils it for me in the morning, I might have to strangle her."

With her head cocked at me, Amelia joined Gina on the couch. "Well, I'm plum out of bail money. So, let's not let that happen."

I left the pan on the counter and leaned against the back of the couch. This wasn't going quite to plan. "I was in jail last night."

With the remote slack in her hand, Gina turned all the way around to look at me. "What did you say?"

"Oh good, so you can hear me." I found myself a bit angry that they both seemed to not care about the confession that was so painful to me. "Remember the murder I said I witnessed?"

Amelia reflected my anger right back at me. "Oh, we remember, but we agreed to attack you for your lies *after* we made up."

Gina put down the remote and curled her legs underneath her on the couch. "Well, if we have to do this."

Again with the guilt. I moved around and sat down on the coffee table. Well, I started it, now there was no stopping the flow. "I'm cursed."

Amelia dropped her head on the back of the couch. "Oh god, I'm too full to be angry."

"That was part of my evil plan."

Gina giggled, though I could feel her nervousness instead of joy.

I had to push ahead before I lost them. "Do you know why I wear gloves?"

"Because of germs," Gina piped up, relief in her voice like she solved the tension and we could go back to our light-hearted evening.

Amelia, on the other hand, leaned forward with her elbows perched on her knees. "But you've never actually said you were a germophobe. I always found that odd."

Without my gloves on, I felt too vulnerable for this conversation. I stood and paced to put more space between us and to help me continue. "That's right, because I didn't want to lie, but I didn't think you'd believe me either. A complete stranger believes me though, and I couldn't fathom that my two best friends wouldn't also know I was telling the truth."

Amelia tried to interrupt, but I froze her comment with a wave of my hand.

"Let me get this out, please." Back to pacing, the words just kind of fell out one after another, my full confession of my curse for them to judge.

My feet stopped as I felt tension in the air change to sadness. Amelia held her head in her hands and was quietly weeping. "I knew it was something. I knew you knew more than you told me when you came over for Thanksgiving when we were still in college. I refused to set the soup course, so Mom handed you the silver spoons, and you dropped the entire box on the floor."

I remembered. The impression was so strong it penetrated right through my gloves.

She looked up at me, over Gina who was holding her as she cried. "You apologized and ran from the kitchen, mumbling about being clumsy. But I'd seen the color fade from your face before you dropped them. You stared at me in horror, like you *knew*."

Tears covered my cheeks as I crouched by Amelia's feet. "I know what he did to you while you clutched that wooden box on the table. I felt it."

Her voice dropped to a whisper. "Why didn't you say something?"

My heart was breaking. "I don't know. I didn't want to invade your privacy or make you relive that nightmare."

I put my cheek on her knee, wishing I could absorb her grief instead of just share it. God bless Gina, because she didn't say a word. She just held us both.

If I was being honest, I needed to put it all out there. "I didn't want you to think I was crazy. I'd never had a friend before, and I kind of liked it."

Amelia laughed as she pushed us off of her. "Well, you still have one, because I believe you."

We both turned to Gina. She pulled her hair from its pony-tail, I assumed to keep her hands busy. She nodded toward the blanket-covered statue in the corner. "What do you see when you touch Walter?"

Amelia whistled, though it sounded weaker than normal.

"Damn, girl, good connection. You were really strange at the shop the other day, Fauna. Is that what was happening? You were —I don't know what to call it—psychically connecting to someone else's memories?"

All of the odd things my friends had seen me do through the years must have been flowing through their minds. I imagined the questions coming for quite a while. Yet, I felt nothing but relief that they both still sat here listening.

I should have done this years ago. Just one more thing I owed Albert Johnson.

"That statue surprised me. I'd never experienced anything like it because every piece is a remnant."

Gina's raised eyebrow asked me to elaborate. So, I told them everything that led me to the Collector's condo.

"And the dead body." Gina chewed on a strand of hair. I could practically see the wheels turning in her mind. "Can you read our thoughts?"

"I cannot. I can't read anyone's thoughts unless it's in one of those remnants. Then I'm immersed and experience exactly what the person who left the memory felt and thought." I looked everywhere except at Amelia. "Sometimes, it's hard to tell where I end and the other person begins."

Amelia leaned over me and picked up her now room temperature souffle and shoved a healthy spoonful in her mouth. She obviously didn't want to dive in any further. "Is there anything else?"

"No."

"Good." Gina grabbed the remote. "Maybe I can still catch the ending."

And just like that, we pretended like everything was fine, and back to normal. I wondered when the other shoe would drop.

A knock on the door made all three of us jump.

Chapter Twenty-One

Before I jumped up to grab the door, I slipped on my gloves. Amelia and Gina exchanged a look. I wondered how long it would take them to adjust to this new truth. In the dim hallway, Flores raised his chin in greeting.

"Detective Flores?" My mind spun with the possibilities of him showing up at my door. "Has there been another one?"

"You don't watch the news, do you?"

I opened my door wider so he could see my girlfriends angled over the back of the couch to get a look at him. "I have company."

He turned to go. "Well, if you're busy."

"No!" That came out much louder than I'd intended. "I can go now."

"Good." Flores absorbed my anxiety with his calm and steady eye contact. "A deal's a deal."

An honorable man stood on my front stoop. He really was going to keep me informed on the case. Maybe he could even use my help. For a moment I wondered if he was single, but the ring on his left hand bespoke of his takenness. It was always the good ones.

Light from inside flashed on the badge around his neck as

Amelia pulled the door open wider. Gina joined her on the other side and whistled.

My face flushed at the appreciative stares of my friends. "Detective, you remember Gina from the gallery. And this is Amelia, the third of our triple threat. Amelia meet Detective Flores." I peeked around the door jamb. "I take it Detective Collins doesn't know you're here."

Flores checked the watch on his wrist. "He's at the crime scene. We should hurry."

Though Flores was on board with my abilities, Collins's attitude toward me said he'd be a much tougher sell. Yet, nothing could upset me at the moment. Amelia and Gina believed me and seemed to take to the idea of my curse pretty readily. After the honeymoon period relaxed, I was sure I'd get more pushback and questions. For now, I'd enjoy the glow and go find this killer.

I grabbed my fully charged phone and turned to my girlfriends. "Will you lock up please?"

Amelia nodded. "I got it."

Gina chewed on her lip as I left with Flores. "Be careful."

"I will." I clomped down the steps behind Flores.

I had to ask the question I'd been avoiding. "Who was it?"

Flores shook his head as he opened the door for me. "You really don't watch the news, do you?" Rather than continue to lecture me, he pulled out his phone and pressed play on a recording of a news broadcast.

In a pants-suit and too much make-up, the African American reporter spoke in a robotic voice that offered no comfort to my fear. "Local fortune teller, Amethyst Redmayne, was found stabbed to death in her business earlier this evening. Police have refused to confirm or deny if this murder is connected to the killing two days ago of beloved psychic personality, George Martinez."

She didn't say anything about Albert Johnson.

"Have you been to the scene yet?"

Flores shook his head. "No, but from what Collins described, I'm not sure it's our guy."

"Why would you say that?"

"I'd rather you see for yourself." He waved at my hands like they were magical tools, which, in some ways, I guess they were. "I want to see what you discover."

The row of businesses in the concrete strip mall included a nail salon, barber shop, pizza joint, and two bars. Among this typical Houston collection, Amethyst's colorful window decorations and fancy sign font existed in a wholly different dimension.

I waited in the car while Flores talked to Collins outside the crime scene. Whatever was said didn't sit right with Collins judging by the way he stomped off to a hysterical woman next to a marked car. With a wave of his hand, Flores called me forward.

After taking a deep breath to quiet my mind before it was invaded by more horror, I joined him in front of the shop. "She wasn't killed at home?"

Flores squinted into the incense-heavy entryway. "It looks like she was camping out in the back room. The address on her license leads to an empty lot on a neighborhood hit hard during the last floods."

My middle brother lost his house at the same time. I sympathized with Amethyst.

Flores held up the badge around his neck to step into the building.

Lots of folklore existed about thresholds and their magical qualities. I was starting to believe some of it was fact, because I sensed nothing outside the doorway. But as soon as I crossed into the palm reader's storefront, a wave of heavy anger washed over me and I immediately felt threatened. My arms gripped my elbows as if afraid to extend out and touch the source of the fury. I hadn't felt anything like this at the other scenes.

I gagged as the metallic taste of blood flooded my mouth. I felt like I was choking on it. This scene was fresh, not drenched in decomposition like the other two. At the moment, I wasn't sure which was worse.

One of the crime scene guys gave me an aggressive look. His emotions were but a whiff of annoyance above the true ferocity of the anger dripping from the walls. My entire digestive system flared in agony as the emotion attacked me physically. I hadn't even gotten to the actual scene of the crime yet. I shook as I tried to fight the tension in my gut that wrecked me like the worst food poisoning possible. If this kept up, I'd be useless. Flores might never let me come back.

Without asking permission, I removed a glove and wrapped my hand around Flores's wrist. My stomach muscles unclenched in phases from my throat all the way down my torso. Flores's calm confidence soothed the angry onslaught like the most effective Pepto Bismol available.

To his credit, the man didn't flinch at my touch or rush me forward. After I established my mom's hymn as a loud barrier around myself, I released Flores with a grateful nod. "Did you find a Collector piece here?"

"Not yet." The detective pushed the crime scene guy aside, either not noticing or choosing to ignore the way he looked at me.

As I turned the corner into the back room, my head rammed into a solid wall and I bounced back a step. Flores caught me with a hand behind my back. I blinked tears from my eyes and realized there was no physical wall in front of me, just the opening to the backroom, much like at my store.

Flores's stable stance didn't flinch as he twisted in front of me, blocking the full scene. "Are you sure this is what you want?"

"Yep." He couldn't read my emotions, right? I would have said anything he needed to hear to keep me here. "I just want to find this guy and end this torment."

As I moved around Flores, I realized the sheer anger left in the room was so strong it coated the walls and stained the very air. That was what I'd run into. This was different from the other scenes. This killer was furious. Collins might be right. This might not be the same man. Though the church hymn kept me from shitting my pants, my abdomen still ached.

I kind of wished I had one of the blankets that covered Walter to build a barrier between me and the embodiment of evil that left his mark here. The floor was covered in blood, pieces of human flesh were strewn upon a hanging cat calendar and a gaudy incense burner, and the stereotypical lamp hung with beads. I'd seen cleaner slaughterhouses.

I closed my eyes and breathed through my mouth. Though my stomach wanted to rebel, I wasn't about to prove judgmental crime scene guy right and vomit on the floor. I needed to make an assessment and get the hell out of there.

"He was beyond angry, more than furious. He was frustrated and surprised and—" I closed my eyes to help block the horror, to actually get into his mind, "—loathing, I think." A burning in my shoulders and tension in my neck usually combined frustration with aversion.

Flores shoved his hands in his pocket. "Are there any memories?"

I whispered to Flores, while keeping half an eye on the disapproving officer behind us, "I probably have to touch her. After what she's been through, her body will hold the freshest impression."

Bile rose into my throat. I half hoped Flores would refuse my request. I never imagined touching one dead body, let alone two in less than a week.

He stared into my eyes like he could do a bit of mind reading himself. Then he walked into the hallway. "We're going to need a few minutes. Everyone, step back."

I stared at the calendar for August that featured a pair of orange kitties playing in a green field full of dandelions. It would be peaceful if not for the bit of skull clung to it.

I rubbed my hand over my forehead as Flores reentered the room. He seemed so calm and centered in the midst of the carnage.

"How do you do it?" I asked him.

He didn't ask "do what?" I could tell by the way he took in the room with a sweep of his eyes, he knew what I was asking. "It's my job."

I wasn't satisfied with that answer, but I had enough mysteries to solve without adding another. The experienced detective bent down and put plastic covers on my shoes like a parent tending to a child.

I moved toward the armchair where a large, dry spot on the floor left me a small, unstained place to stand within touching distance of the mutilated corpse which I'd avoided looking at directly until now. I thought the last victim had been torn to pieces. In comparison, he'd been surgically sliced and mercifully put down. That was a kindness compared to Amethyst's treatment. This woman, with gray, streaked hair and wrinkles—accentuated by her make-up, instead of hidden by it—had been brutalized. Half of her head was missing. She had fingers torn off. Her insides were mixed together like a stew, which explained the smell of sewage that overwhelmed the copper of the blood.

I would never watch another horror movie. This was not entertainment.

"Here." Flores handed me something in a small vial. "Smear some under your nose."

The fresh smell of peppermint calmed my stomach. It helped, but it only masked the horrors highlighted with my other senses. It reminded me of cherry-flavored cough syrup. A bit of sweetness fooled you only through the first whiff, after that, it burned all the way down.

While shoving one glove into my pocket, I stared at the palm reader's left ear. Somehow, it had escaped the carnage unscathed and clean. Touching it wouldn't hurt me. Anything I saw was all in my head, anyway. I could do this. My shaking fingers ignored my internal pep talk and tried to betray my own emotions more than sensing the ones of the killer. His anger still hovered around me, but I needed to know more. Internally, I cranked my mother's voice to extra high. I'd done this more in four days than I had the entire previous year. I think I could separate myself better this time.

At least, I hoped I could.

When the tips of my fingers brushed her ear lobe, all I felt was pain. I screamed as her voice echoed in my mind. A man leaned over her. His scarred arm flashed up and down so fast, there was no way he was thinking about what he was doing at all. Jewelry flashed on his finger, a wedding ring maybe. My mother's voice insulated me only enough for me to recognize Amethyst's inability to focus on her attacker. Tears blurred her vision as her body jumped at each blow of the blade.

"Fake! Goddamn con artist!" Blue eyes, burning fiercer than any red fire, burrowed into his victim's memory.

His nose was thin and straight. His eyebrows looked groomed. Between the gore dripping from his face and Amethyst's tunnel vision as she weakened, I still couldn't give an accurate description.

I had no doubt, however, that it was the same killer.

It was *his* anger that filled this place, but I didn't get even a little from Amethyst. Albert and George had both reflected the killer's joy back to him. But not Amethyst. She couldn't sense him.

Holy shit.

She wasn't cursed.

Chapter Twenty-Two

C oncern washed over the hot pain as someone grabbed my shoulders and pulled me out of the impression. Air filled my lungs in ragged gasps, relaxing the tightness of Amethyst's chest when blood filled in the cavity. I leaned into the warm arms of Detective Flores, soaking up his calming presence, as I tried to get my emotions back into check.

"You were screaming. I couldn't leave you like..."

I swallowed bile that threatened to sicken the scene further and pushed against the doorframe to the hallway. I couldn't even remember the tune to Mom's hymn.

As he released me, I felt cold and had to resist the urge to fall back into his embrace. "It's the same killer." As soon as I said it out loud, I was certain. With complete clarity, I also knew I had to get away from the hovering anger beast that threatened to overwhelm me.

Without looking at any of the people staring me down, I headed straight for the door. Usually, stepping out into the humidity of Texas in August took my breath away. This time, it was like I could breathe again. With both hands on my knees, I closed my eyes and inhaled. The flurry of knife blows filled my mind. I jumped up and opened my eyes and paced on the cracked sidewalk. "Definitely the same guy."

"How do you know?" Flores led me without touching a single bit of skin toward his car.

"I saw him. Well, as much as Amethyst could see of him. Those blue eyes. Scars on his forearm." That made me remember my bare ones. The comforting leather left my pocket and engulfed my hands. The practiced movement and the tight feel over my skin brought back a measure of calm to my emotions. I had to separate mine from Amethyst's. Though a moment ago, they were one and the same.

Flores opened the door to the Ford for me. "I'll have you talk to a sketch artist. You might have better details this time."

"I can try, but I don't think it will help." I flopped in the large seat. The seat belt reached across my chest before I knew what I was doing. Instinctive. Like protecting myself from horrible emotions, like the ones I was just exposing myself to on purpose.

What in the hell was I doing? Sharing their pain won't bring them back. The killer's anger was only growing. I thought about his precise slicing of the last victim compared to the out-of-control rage this time.

And she never laughed. Her emotions were abject terror mingled with pain then back to terror. Not a single reflection of what the killer was feeling. Plus, he'd called her a fake. How would he know? He targeted the cursed; I couldn't deny that fact. Maybe since Amethyst only pretended to be one, he didn't get the high he was searching for. "She wasn't like us." Oh man, could I say us? "That's what was different. He was furious, because she didn't reflect his joy at what he was doing. That's what he's looking for."

Flores started the car. "He's targeting people who can sense emotions."

Having someone else believe me so readily still sounded inauthentic to my ears. "Don't make fun of me." I wanted to leave the car and get an Uber, but one look at the house and the stretcher made me stay where I was. "Take me home please."

Flores adjusted his mirrors—as if anyone else had driven his car. "I had an aunt who knew things." Flores's voice was laced with a quiet confessional tone. "I wasn't like my brother or the rest of my cousins. She knew as soon as she held me that first time we visited her in Mexico. She told me it would be tough, but it's alright because it's just the way that I was made. Love whomever you love."

Oh, Flores was gay. I hadn't picked up on his sexuality at all. I hadn't sensed any lust from him at all—which was more rare than one might think—to point me in one direction or another. Though I had to mentally chastise myself since I noticed his ring and assumed he was married to a woman.

My curiosity peaked as he continued, "Tía Maria did this with every family member. She would give you a hug when you came into her home, and she'd somehow know exactly what you were feeling and exactly what you needed to hear." Flores stared out the window. Though he was driving, I felt like he was purposely not looking me in the eye. "I think she was like you."

"So, your tía, she's not with us anymore?"

His nod, along with pressure behind my eyes, verified my guess.

"I'm sorry for your loss. It would have been nice to talk with her, to see how she dealt with it all."

After everything that had happened this week, I still hadn't met a single other person like me.

I blinked and imitated Flores's stare out the windshield. "You really do believe me."

"I do."

Tears dripped from my eyes and I didn't even try to stop them. The anxiety mixed with hope mixed with horror of the last few days was enough to make anyone breakdown. But a stranger truly believed me? That puts three people in the know in less than twenty-four hours.

Yet, somehow this killer was able to track us down. Though he was wrong about Amethyst. "So, if we find out how he's finding the cursed..."

"We could find our next victim."

Chapter Twenty-Three

The next morning, I found my way to Chipped out of routine rather than conscious thought. I'd spent my whole life thinking I was the only cursed one. I was wrong. There were at least a handful in Houston alone. Now a psychopath had managed to root them out, though he did choose wrong once. A psychic and a palm reader might have been logical choices, but why an artist? Was the murderer one of us, and he was called by one of Albert's statues? If so, why didn't he know immediately that Amethyst couldn't sense emotions?

When I opened the door to the shop, I pushed the existential concerns aside to concentrate on store business. After neglecting Chipped for a few days, there was a ton to keep me busy. The voicemails alone would be daunting, judging by the flashing number on the store laptop. I'd have to remind Jeff that checking those was part of his job.

I stepped on a half-eaten bag of crackers as I made my way to the back. "Dammit, Jeff. No wonder your wife is always mad at you. If you treat your place of employment like this, what must your personal space look like?"

Peeking his head around the corner of the break room where

he obviously spent the night again, Jeff shrugged, completely unmoved by my reprimand.

"Come out. It's tidy-up day. Again."

"But I have to—"

"Listen to your boss before you have to explain all the other stuff that hasn't gotten done in the past two days."

Jeff sniffed and rubbed his forehead. "Okay. Let me take a piss."

"While you're in there, you can scrub the bathroom. You use it way more than I do, and I shouldn't smell it as soon as I open the door to the back." It felt good to have control of something again.

He grumbled, but I knew he'd do it. He never chose to do anything on his own, but if he got a direct order, he followed it.

I worked through lunch, completing orders and returning calls, without a single walk-in. Slow for a Friday, but I appreciated the quiet after the week I'd had. Jeff had moved on to a server with a nasty virus problem. I left him to it as we approached closing.

I grabbed the vacuum to clean up the crackers from earlier. The whir of the suction drowned out any ambient noise, which was why I missed the bell at the door. Out of nowhere to my distracted mind, a woman with her hands on her hips blocked my path. I stopped the vacuum before I rammed into her expensive-looking shoes. Struggling to find the off button, I ended up just pulling the cord from the wall instead.

A stray hair fell over my eye and I pushed it behind my ear, trying to look composed and not startled at all. "Can I help you?"

She dropped her angry demeanor and took on a desperate expression. "I hope so. My phone has locked up and I really need it."

I smiled, trying to comfort her. But I didn't need anyone else's emotions right now. My head felt clear and I wanted it to stay that way. "Set it on the counter please, and I'll have a look."

The vacuum wheels stuck a bit in the freshly fluffed carpet as I hauled it away. The woman tapped on the glass of the counter with a perfectly manicured nail. Whatever she did for a living, it wasn't physical labor with those unmarred hands. I pushed a work order form and a pen at her. "Please write your code in the blank under the phone model name."

Her left hand continued to drum on the glass while she filled out her information. "It's very old school for an electronic repair shop, don't you think?"

"Sometimes, those things fail us. Which is job security for me." I tried to lighten the mood, but Heather, from what she wrote on the form, was not in the mood for levity.

Her shoulders rocked as her hand moved to rubbing her forehead. "There's just a lot of vital stuff on there like my meetings and contacts and I never backed it up because I couldn't figure out how to do that and..."

From under the counter, I grabbed my Bluetooth keyboard and the proper cords for her phone. "It's alright. That's what we're here for. Hopefully, it's just the screen which is true in most cases, and we'll get you settled in a couple hours."

Her phone didn't respond to my fingers at all. I tried turning it off and back and on and the screen remained frozen.

As I went through my usual diagnostics, Heather dropped the pen on the paper and took to pacing a line in the freshly vacuumed carpet. "I need my calendar. I can't function without it."

"Is it a Google calendar or attached to your Outlook account? You can access it from your email." After making sure he didn't have anything inappropriate open on his browser, I turned Jeff's laptop around for Heather to login to her accounts.

Heather smiled at me for the first time. "I didn't think of that." Her fingernails clicked in rhythm on the keys. "Yes! It's in Google. Oh, thank god. You just saved me."

My fingers or toes didn't tickle, which told me her voice sounded happy, but she wasn't feeling it. The reduced tension in my neck, however, reflected Heather's lessened stress. At least I was somewhat helpful.

Her phone looked to be functioning under the broken screen as well. "And it does look like it's just the screen. We can have this ready for you by the morning."

"I'll be back first thing Saturday then." Her hand landed on top of mine before I saw it coming. "Thank you. I could probably use a phone-free evening anyway."

My body flinched, but, luckily, my gloves served their purpose. Yanking my hand back, I hoped my immediate reach for her paper to give her the pink copy hid my obvious discomfort. Why did people think they could touch anyone they wanted?

Heather seemed to be too relieved to notice my agitation. She waved exuberantly as she left, completely changed from the anxious customer who had entered. "I'll see you in the morning."

Jeff came out of the back, tucking in his shirt. He nodded at Heather's retreating back. "I heard the bell and thought—"

"She needs the screen replaced on her phone."

"Ah, our bread and butter." Jerry stopped at his laptop and scrolled. His eyebrows moved closer and farther apart, but the rest of his face remained unmoved.

"Oh, I had her check her email because she needed access to her calendar immediately." I searched the boxes behind the counter for the proper screen.

Jeff shook his head. "I can see that. This woman is way over scheduled. I'm surprised she didn't stand here pacing while you fixed her phone. Ooh, and she has some sort of secret rendezvous."

Scoffing at his nosiness, I turned his laptop around so I could log Heather off. "Seriously? She's a customer and we don't have the right to..."

Calendars. Something clicked into place in my head. Albert had a calendar with Friday marked every week. I closed my eyes and pictured the kitty calendar on the wall at the fortune teller's house. Definitely the same day was marked on her calendar as well. I couldn't remember what it said. If the psychic, George Martinez, had the same day marked, maybe that was the connection.

"Here." I slid the phone to Jeff. "Get this done for me. I have something to take care of."

"Again?" Jeff asked. "I've closed the store for the last three nights."

"And I haven't charged you rent for your bed in the back." I had Flores's number ringing on my phone before the store door banged shut.

"Flores."

"Hey, I just thought of something. Did George have a calendar with every Friday marked?"

"Let me look through the crime scene photos." A loud keyboard rang through the receiver. "I don't see a calendar on any of these shots."

"What about on his phone?"

More heavy clicking came through the phone. "Tech hasn't gotten to it yet."

"Dammit." I thought I'd found a connection.

"Why are you looking for a calendar?"

It sounded silly now. "Albert Johnson had Friday's marked on his desk calendar, and Amethyst Redmayne had the same days marked on her kitty calendar."

"You've got a good eye." He paused for a minute. "Maybe George Martinez had a calendar in another room? I'll go back and see what we missed."

I shook my head even though I knew he couldn't see me. My mind scoured my memory of George's house. The lampshade and post-it were the only calm bit in the entire scene. "Wasn't there a note on the nightstand about a date with someone? I think it said Friday."

"Yep. It's right here: 7pm Friday Tracy Gee."

I pulled my car keys from my purse in defeat. I needed to get home and open a bottle of wine. I'd really thought I'd found something. But why would all three victims have a date with the same woman? "Okay. I'm sorry for bothering you."

"Fauna, wait." Flores's voice was laced with excitement. "Tracy Gee is a community center. That could be the connection between the victims."

Closer. I was closer to having answers. "They were all meeting there on Fridays?" Could there be others?

"There's only one way to find out. Do you have plans for tonight?"

My keys jingled as I unlocked my car door. "I do now."

Chapter Twenty-Four

I
t was a bit after 7 p.m. twilight had begun, but the parking lot lights hadn't turned on yet. My leg bounced on the floorboard of Flores's car. He wanted to get here after meeting start time so we didn't frighten anyone from entering the building. It was the smart move, but it didn't curb my anxiousness to find answers.

Flores parked in a space by a chain link fence behind the one-story brick building. Collins pulled in beside us.

I repressed a groan. "Did he have to come? He doesn't like me."

"He doesn't like anyone, but he's a good detective." Flores opened the car door. "Collins, will you run license plates to see if we can find anyone associated with our victims?"

Collins wiped sweat from his brow. "Sure. Keep the old man in the sauna while you two head into the air conditioning."

Flores ignored his partner's sarcasm and motioned me to the door of the community center.

Alone most of my life, it was weird to trust someone else. To get to the truth, I had to start somewhere. "How do we know where to go?"

Flores held the swinging door open for me. "You're the one with this special ability. You tell me."

My eyes widened as I considered using my powers on purpose. It certainly wouldn't be the first time this week, but I didn't think it was necessary here. "I'm pretty sure it's an AA meeting. Maybe there's a schedule posted?" If others drank as much as I did to drown the curse, I could totally believe *that* was where they'd find each other.

Before I changed my mind, I walked into the building. Mildew floated in the air from the threadbare carpet, like in every other building older than a decade in Houston. A corkboard posted the schedule and room reservations. I didn't see anything that said AA meeting. An HOA meeting for a neighborhood I'd never heard of, a Girl Scout meeting, and a club of some sort were the only things posted for tonight.

Flores took the hallway of closed doors while I headed to the larger room.

The big open space with those old-fashioned pull-out walls was divided into three sections. One held the HOA meeting with mostly older couples arguing over something they felt very passionately about. The next one held a half dozen people who huddled together in a tight circle of metal chairs.

At first, I thought they were praying, but one of the ladies sat straight up and made eye contact with me. Her head tilted and she smiled in the most welcome grin I'd ever seen. A white woman dressed in a business jacket and tight pencil skirt turned around. She looked familiar.

She asked the old woman with the welcoming smile, "Are you sure, Belinda?"

In response, Belinda stood from her chair and patted the back. She seemed to be inviting me to sit down. Something very strange was happening.

I contemplated calling for Flores, but thought I'd get more answers before frightening them with a cop. "Is this the AA meeting?"

"Not exactly," the professional woman said. "Though we are a support group of sorts. And judging by Belinda's reaction, I know you belong here."

A black man with red-rimmed eyes crossed his arms. "I don't think we should be inviting strangers, not after... "

Something about his demeanor and the immediate inclusion of Belinda made me realize I was in the right group. I knew what to say, "Albert Johnson's death."

"Murder, you mean," interjected an African woman in a kaftan and glee, whose bright colors contradicted her dark anger. "I agree with Rodney. Now's not a good time."

My butt touched the cold metal before I'd decided to sit. "So, you do know him. Albert Johnson."

I studied the group of mixed race and gender. Their grief floated in the air like fog with fear just on the outskirts. Each of them, except for the woman in the white pencil skirt, wore gloves.

That woman with fair skin and very short, blonde hair introduced herself, her voice soft but confident. "My name is Debra, and you are?"

"Fauna." I thought about Flores again, but hoped he'd give me time. I wasn't ready to share this revelation.

Debra's gentle face made me want to confess all of my pain, everything I'd been through in the past few days. Instead, I just listened as she talked.

"We are all—special—here. Albert brought us together through his art. That's why he called himself the Collector."

"That's how I found him. Through a statue that screamed at me from the many remnants that made it." I scanned the faces as they all turned to me. "You're all cursed?"

Debra tapped a foot. "Cursed? You've been alone a long time, haven't you?" Amusement and concern took turns crossing her expression. I couldn't feel them though. Come to think of it, everyone felt a bit muted. "We prefer the term empath as it describes both our unusual gift and our sensibilities."

Gift? She called this horrible ability that tortured me my whole life a gift?

A Latinx man, who appeared no older than a high schooler, crossed his legs and leaned over them. "We can all sense the emotions of others. Some of us, however," he nodded to Belinda who stood by a window, "can do much more."

"Enrique is right." The group seemed to be comfortable with Debra speaking for them. "Some of us can read emotions if we're close enough." She raised her hand and so did a few others. "Some of us can read them if we have skin-to-skin contact." Others in the group raised their hands. She indicated Belinda. "One of us can sense others of our kind without any physical contact."

Holy shit. All of these people really *were* like me. "I'm not..."

The entire group spoke together, "...the only one."

My cheeks burned at the implication. "Can you read minds too?"

"No," Debra rubbed her own leg.

I knew that move. I did it myself when I wanted to physically touch someone else but didn't want the emotional baggage that came with it.

She continued, "We've all said that exact phrase upon meeting the others."

My toes tingled and my fingertips went numb. In less than a week, I'd gone from thinking I was a freak, a weirdo, from believing no one would ever understand, that I'd have to hide this part of me forever so they didn't lock me up in an insane asylum, to finding myself welcomed by a group of strangers who understood me better than Gina and Amelia, who had known me all of my adult life. My brain was on spin mode as I moved from one set of eyes to the next, unable to form any real thoughts. Then I remembered where I'd seen Debra before.

"You were at the precinct talking to Detective Flores about Albert."

She looked puzzled. "I was. My husband and I had been at

his show the night before. Ron reacted like a true cretin and confronted Albert in front of everyone. I had to assure the detectives investigating his death that my husband had nothing to do with the Collector's death."

"Ron? Ron Elstin?" More pieces plopped into place, as the angry man at the gallery being arrested by Detective Collins flashed to the forefront of my mind. "Your husband thought you were having an affair with Albert. But you weren't, were you?"

"I don't know how you know this, but I wasn't having an affair." Debra leaned back and crossed her arms. "My husband doesn't understand. He thinks I'm a talented psychiatrist. I tried to tell him one day, but let's just say he couldn't wrap his mind around what I was explaining, so I caved and told him I was trained to read people. I met Albert at one of his shows where he always brought along Belinda, just in case. She gave me a pink rose when I came in, which was the symbol between the two of them." She smiled weakly at the older woman. "Belinda doesn't talk, you see."

"You were coming to these meetings with him, and your husband thought there was something more going on?" Maybe I was wrong, but infidelity was a pretty good motive for killing someone. No wonder he looked so suspicious.

"My demeanor definitely changed when Albert was around, and my husband, without any gifts of his own, sensed it. After how badly the first time went, I wasn't eager to tell him the truth. I just kept denying. Until..."

Belinda slid down the wall beside the window. The African woman joined her on the floor and offered the distraught Belinda a bottle of water.

"You bought one of his pieces from the art show. I was there when your husband tried to return it."

"Thank you, Ademi." Debra nodded, though her gaze stayed on Belinda. "You mean you were there the day my idiot husband lost his temper and then was arrested? He didn't kill Albert. He can't even discipline the dog when it has an accident on the floor. There's no way he did... well, what was done to the Collector."

"Albert's pieces? Can any of you sense the memories impressed upon them?" No one had mentioned that power.

A curly haired woman who looked to be in her thirties with the roundness that comes with age raised her hand. "I'm Margaret Truman. I found a piece in an art gallery in Katy. It led me to his condo."

Debra tilted her head at Rodney, who still had his arms crossed. "Didn't you find us through a piece?"

He nodded. "A buddy of mine, with more money than sense, brought home a god-awful frame made of all kinds of garbage. I couldn't walk into his house, because the damn thing screamed with memories." His hands dropped to his lap. "But it led me to this group."

Out of the corner of my eye, I noticed Flores leaned against a set of cabinets on the opposite wall where he could see into all of the partitioned spaces. Time to connect the dots. "Was George Martinez a member of this group?"

"He was new," Enrique answered. "I saw him perform a show and knew he was one of us. I gave him a post-it with the time and place. He'd only attended a couple meetings."

I didn't need empathic abilities to see the angry tension in his muscles. "What about Amethyst Redmayne, the palm reader?"

Belinda kicked her feet on the ground.

Adam answered for her. "Amethyst wasn't actually an empath. Belinda tried to tell the Collector, but he didn't want to turn anyone away. Whether she had powers or not, Amethyst believed she did and obviously needed our group."

I couldn't share everything. If I started, it would all come tumbling out and I'm not sure I could stand up again after being drained like that. "I have to warn you. I think someone is targeting you, I mean, us." Okay, that was weird.

Debra pushed her bangs out of her eyes in a casual move she

probably did a hundred times a day. "That was our topic of discussion tonight. It's too much to believe that all of this death is a mere coincidence."

Too much to believe? This entire scenario was too much to believe. "We'd noticed the connection too." I motioned toward Flores, who stared at the HOA meeting on the other side of the barrier. "He's a detective with HPD. He knows what I can do, and he believes me. Would you be willing to talk to him?"

Belinda hid her head behind her knees.

With a glance around at the lost souls the Collector had weaved together, I couldn't let this monster tear them apart for his perverse pleasure. "We need to share all we know so we can catch this man before he targets another one of us."

Taking a deep breath to make sure I could stand without shaking, I gained my feet and motioned Flores into the room. His immediate reaction told me he'd been paying attention to me the entire time, even if his eyes had been focused on the other group. I wondered how much he'd overheard.

Debra stood up and shook hands with the detective. "Detective Flores, it's good to see you again, though not under these circumstances."

I marveled again over her ability to touch him without gloves and not be swept away out of control into someone else's state of mind. Whatever method she used to keep herself centered was significantly stronger than the hymn I repeated. Maybe she could teach me.

He tilted his head after taking out his phone for notes. "Why didn't you tell me about this group, Debra? I could have protected you."

"Why would I think you'd believe me? Plus, at that time, it was only the Collector who was the victim, and as big of a loss as his death is to all of us, one death does not a pattern make."

"Fair point." Flores acquiesced. "Have you seen anything suspicious: someone following you, odd friend requests, someone trying to get an invite to this meeting, anything at all out of the ordinary?"

As Flores asked his questions, I backed up to where he'd been observing us. My tongue stuck to the top of my mouth. I remembered there was a water fountain near the entrance. As I walked past the HOA meeting, a guy in a red sports hat bumped into me. Fear poured from him in waves, tensing the muscles in my arms.

"Excuse me," I said, even though he ran into me.

When he looked up, a flash of blue froze my muscles. I relaxed as I realized the blue was the rim of his glasses. His eyes were a nondescript hazel. But there was something familiar about him. "Do I know you?" My voice shook from the shock of the stranger's touch and strong emotion.

Flores must have had half an eye on me, because he was by my side before I could form another thought. "Can I help you, sir?"

With a hand on the brim of his hat, the man shook his head as he dashed for the door, mumbling under his breath.

Flores raised an eyebrow at me.

My arms crossed my chest as I tried to discern where I'd seen the hat guy before. "It's not the killer, but I'm sure I've seen him before. Recently."

Flores nodded at me and took after the man.

I spared a glance at the group, the people who were like me. "Watch out for each other. We'll get the guy. I promise."

Before I changed my mind and sat back down with the empaths, I jogged after Flores. At least I knew where I'd be every Friday from now on.

I really wasn't alone.

Chapter Twenty-Five

The door hadn't closed all the way as I pushed through behind Flores. Around a large, brick wall bordering an outdoor patio, the streetlamps lit the full parking lot with an orange glow. Red Hat wove around a large vehicle and bumped right into Collins's impressive bulk.

Not expecting Flores to slow, I ran into his back. He caught me as I stumbled forward. I got a wisp of eagerness and determination. After he was sure I was stable, he removed his hands immediately. The absence of his touch left me feeling empty when he removed it. I didn't even know I could have that kind of reaction. I'd probably been giving my friends the cold shoulder for too long. I don't know why they put up with me at all.

"Sorry," I mumbled, as we continued toward the red hat man who was bouncing on his toes looking at Collins then us.

Collins had his jacket pulled up, exposing his holstered weapon on his belt. "This guy ran into me at a full clip. That's assaulting an officer. Shall I handcuff him?"

Red Hat's eyes were as large as a bunny's being hunted by a fox. He didn't say a word.

Flores moved behind him, in between a mini-van and a dark

blue BMW. Red Hat would have to go over the hood of the smaller car to get away from them, and I doubted he'd have the agility before Collins snagged him.

Flores's quieter voice sounded much more reasonable than the gruff Collins. "I'm sure he didn't mean any harm. If he can answer a few questions, we can clear this all up."

In my head, I could imagine the two of them playing good cop-bad cop, though I wasn't sure it was an act at all.

"I have nothing to say." Red Hat's voice surprised me with how high-pitched it was. Under the orange glow of the nighttime parking lot, I marveled at how young he looked. I bet he got carded whenever he went out for a drink. His clothes looked like something Gina's nephew would wear, athletic shorts and a loose T-shirt with trendy sneakers and ankle socks. Yet, I knew from our brush that he was no kid.

"Do I know you?" I had to ask. The familiarity without context was driving me crazy. I really hoped he wasn't some athlete I saw on TV or something, and my overworked brain placed him as someone I should know. Of course, at this point, I'd run into so many familiar people that I couldn't place, I might have to call it my new curse. Apparently, I needed to pay more attention to the people I encounter.

Red Hat shook his head, but didn't quite look me in the eye. "I'm just going to go now. I haven't done anything wrong, and you can't hold me."

Collins and Flores exchanged a look I would have missed if I wasn't so tuned in to every little action.

Collins grabbed Red Hat by the elbow. "Not so fast, man. You assaulted an officer, and I'm going to have to take you in for questioning. You can't just go around willy-nilly hitting cops."

"I didn't hit you." Red Hat's cheeks brightened to the color of his cap.

"Well, Flores here saw you. As did our civilian witness, right?"

I crossed my arms and raised my chin in what I hoped was an

accusing glare. Collins hadn't always rubbed me the right way, but I was starting to see how his rough tactics could prove useful in a murder investigation.

Red Hat sputtered but came up with no further objections. Collins cuffed him and stuck him in his back seat on the other side of the minivan.

Flores took out his phone and pulled up the note taking app I'd grown accustomed to seeing reflected on his face. "I'll question the HOA and see if they recognized him."

Collins opened his car door. "I'll get his ID and search the records while I wait for a squad car to bring him in. Meet you at the station."

At the precinct, I observed the suspect from the same two-way mirror I'd watched the coach confess. I strained to place him. He wasn't the guy with the stolen computer. What other young-looking guys had I come across lately?

I poured some water and tried to distract myself as Collins and Flores questioned him.

Collins put the man's driver's license flat on the table. "Gregory Willis, 415 Harrison Street, Tomball. Is this address still correct?"

Even the name didn't jog anything.

Gregory nodded while his nose twitched. I couldn't sense any emotions from this distance, but I could tell he was hiding something. What was I missing?

Flores leaned against the table casually, like he was sharing a beer with the guy. "So, what were you doing at an HOA meeting for a neighborhood that's not yours?"

Gregory Willis wiped his hand across his nose. "My mom lives in that neighborhood. I was looking out for her interests."

"Really?" Collins imitated Gregory's casual confidence by leaning back in his chair and crossing his arms. "You're such a good son. I bet you frequently visit the neighborhood, don't you? And help out the older group with errands and lawn maintenance."

Gregory loosened up and pushed his hat a little higher on his forehead. "As much as I can with work and family and such."

Flores looked at the mirror as he said, "Then how come none of those residents had ever seen you before?"

"I don't know. They're old. How good is their eyesight?" Gregory leaned forward with a smile across his face as if he'd just gained the upper hand.

I didn't notice anything shift, but the detectives must have because they both stood up.

"Let's call my mom. She'll verify." He pulled his hat off with a twist of his left wrist and tossed it on the metal table. With his right hand, he combed through his bangs, spiking them up from their flattened position.

My stomach lurched. I recognized that exact move—from an impression. Gregory had been younger, and he didn't have the blue glasses. That's why I couldn't identify him right away. I banged on the glass. Flores looked through the mirror, then grabbed his door handle at the same time as I did mine.

As I met Flores in the hallway, I had trouble catching my breath as the full extent of the scumbag they held in the interrogation room filled my emotions. "Do you have items from the Collector's house?"

"If you mean the stuff you tossed around his condo, yes. We brought them all into evidence when you found that ledger." Flores stepped back as Collins opened the door to the interrogation room with a notebook in his hand. "We connected the numbers that were tagged on some of the items to multiple entries in the ledger, but we don't know what it means."

"I need to see them. Your suspect is connected to one. That's where I saw him before."

Flores's gaze fell to my hands, but he addressed his partner.

"Collins, Fauna and I are going to follow a hunch. Can you keep him occupied for a bit?"

Collins waved the notebook. "I've got an old lady to call. I'm sure it could take much longer than expected."

Flores took off at a steady clip to a hallway that lead to a set of stairs. My thighs burned as we hit the last step of three flights. I wasn't as fit as I thought I was. Maybe it was time to hit those machines included in my association fees.

In an attempt to slow Flores down so I could catch my breath, I leaned on my knees, and asked, "What? No elevator?"

Flores held a glass door open for me. "This way is quicker."

"Easy for you to say."

My head felt so light, I almost forgot why we were here. Flores showed his badge and signed a sheet. The civilian behind the window buzzed a door into a back room. Flores waved me in before I had any time to think about where we were heading. The shelves and cardboard boxes looked straight out of *Law and Order*. It had to be the evidence room.

Which meant, pieces of crimes—many of them violent and emotionally charged—sat in boxes on every shelf.

"I don't know if I should be in here."

"It's okay. I vouched for you."

My steps became small, and my arms plastered against my chest. I didn't want to accidentally touch anything and get over-whelmed by someone else's trauma.

When he saw my face, Flores stopped mid-step. "Are you okay?"

Over the threshold, I glanced up at a cage separating us from the boxes of evidence. I could feel the hum I associated with Walter at this point, but it was subtle, like a buzzing fan. "If I can stay on this side of that cage, I'll be fine."

"No problem. We're not going in there at all." Flores guided me to a table in one corner where uniformed officers were already laying out boxes and removing lids.

My muscles relaxed as I realized I wouldn't be within touching distance of every crime from the city of Houston.

"Where do you want to start?" His complete openness at my ability filled me with confidence.

Leaning over the first open box, I quickly dismissed those items. I didn't remember touching any of them. By the third box, I started to doubt my own memory. "I was stupid drunk when I did this the first time." I rubbed my forehead with my gloved hands. "I might have to touch everything again."

Flores accepted the ledger from one of the officers. "Before you go that far, can you remember anything from any of these items? We matched all the ones from the apartment with entries in the ledger, but we're not sure what the letters stand for in these two columns or what the rest of these numbers are in these three columns."

With my eyes closed, I tried to see through the drunken anger of that evening. "They were all horrible memories. Pain and abuse and deceit and..."

One of the boxes had the fountain pen I remembered holding. "Like this one, it was used to sign a will against the dying person's wishes."

Flores pulled out the pen, saving me the action. He matched the number in the ledger. "I've got it here. There are multiple entries for the same item." He flipped through a couple pages. "The dates look like it's a once a year entry."

"Payments?"

Slowly, Flores cocked his head and looked at me. "You think the Collector was blackmailing these people?"

"Why else would he keep these horrendous memories and a secret ledger?" I shifted to search the next box. "Not that any court of law is going to believe *how* he knew about the criminal's misdeeds."

Flores leaned over the ledger. "People have been murdered for far less."

Sticking out of the final box were two rounded, fluffy ears.

Without touching it, the memory of a terrified little girl clutching the teddy bear flooded my senses. That was it. That was how I knew him. The hat flip and the bangs straightening all matched. Gregory Willis had molested a little girl, and Albert had made him pay.

Hesitant to touch it again, I pointed instead. "That's it. That teddy bear. He's on it, but it's not his memory. He did unspeakable things to a little girl. Based on his comfort level in the remnant, it wasn't a one-time thing."

As Flores pulled the teddy bear from the evidence box, his hand trembled as if he could feel the pain woven into the fabric like I could.

I brushed a tear from my cheek. "My vision doesn't offer much evidence."

He closed the ledger and tucked it under his arm. "It's enough to get a confession." His emotionally heavy voice gave me hope in a happy ending.

Chapter Twenty-Six

From the dark side of the two-way mirror, my attention remained transfixed on Flores as he stormed into the interrogation room. Without asking a single question, Flores set down a cardboard box, just like the evidence boxes. He pulled out the heavy ledger and dropped it on the table. Gregory jumped in his seat as if every tightly strung muscle sprung at the same time. Flores opened the book to a bright pink arrow Post-It, then he flipped the page to another, then another.

So far, Flores hadn't said a word.

Gregory squinted at the rows of numbers and letters. His mouth dropped open, but he quickly recovered his tough guy act and glared at Flores. "What are all those numbers? Can you even keep holding me without charging me with anything?"

Collins came through right on cue. "Sorry, I'm late. The printer was out of paper." He handed Flores a stack of printouts. All I could make out from my vantage point was a bank logo at the top.

What little color there was drained from Gregory's face when Flores smiled down at him and set the bank statements on top of the ledger.

Flores still hadn't said a word. This guy would drive me crazy with the no questions. Apparently, it worked on Gregory as well.

"Look, those are donations to a youth program." Sweat dripped from his forehead and beaded at the tip of his nose. "I have no idea why you've brought me in to ask me about my charity."

Damn, he had an answer for everything, didn't he? The image of the little girl popped into my head, and all I wanted to do was strangle him. I didn't know how Flores was able to keep his cool when he knew damn well the guy was lying.

Collins straddled the chair he had been sitting in before. "So," he turned over the bank statement so he could read it, "$5000 every other month or so for a youth program? I'm a public servant myself and that kind of donation would leave me homeless quick. How much does an elementary school principal make exactly?"

At that bit of info, my knees bent and almost collapsed. I sat down before I fell down. This sicko was exposed to children on a daily basis, and Albert *knew*. Instead of reporting the pedophile, he cashed in on the knowledge. What kind of man was the illusive Collector?

Sweat beaded on Gregory's already pale forehead. "We're a private school..."

Apparently, Flores had had enough of the suspect's bullshit. He pulled out the teddy bear from the evidence box and set it gently on the table, like it was a delicate heirloom.

Gregory's mouth popped open. His hands dropped into his lap.

"How did you?" His eyes roamed from the stuffed animal to the two detectives to the ledger. He couldn't seem to organize his lies any longer.

Why didn't Flores go at him now? Why did he just stand there, staring?

With a flip of the tag tied around a fuzzy foot, Flores placed the number next to a Post-It marked spot on the ledger. Collins arranged the bank statement to a column next to it. I couldn't read them from the other side of the mirror, but I suspected those numbers matched up. They had him. They had proof he was being blackmailed. Why didn't the detectives yell or argue or bully him into confessing? This wasn't like TV at all. My fingers dug into my upper arms as I resisted the urge to dive into the interrogation with everything I'd seen.

Somehow, the intense stares worked.

Gregory's head fell into his hands. "He was blackmailing me. Somehow he knew what she said about me." His head shot up and his bloodshot eyes pleaded. "I didn't hurt her. I could never hurt her, but I knew no one would understand."

Collins exchanged a confused look with Flores. His partner put him off with an almost imperceptible shake of his head.

Interesting. Flores hadn't shared my insight with Collins. I rubbed my hands on my sore arms from all the squeezing. Of course, Flores didn't tell him anything. His source was a nut job.

Collins jumped back on track. "Is that why you killed the Collector? To make the payments stop?"

All of Gregory's muscles tensed as he shot straight backed in his chair. "Killed? I didn't kill anyone."

Flores spoke for the first time. "How did you know he would be at the Tracy Gee?"

"I've got some friends who tracked the IP address from the blackmail emails to the WiFi at that center. Since I didn't know his real name or where he lived, it was my best bet to confront the man I only knew as the Collector and make him give up whatever evidence he had." Gregory cocked his head at the teddy bear as if trying to interpret how the stuffed animal functioned as evidence. "But then I heard that woman call you 'detective' and I freaked out. I still don't know what the Collector looks like. You should be arresting him for blackmail."

Flores cocked his head at the suspect. "Well, that's a bit difficult since he's been murdered."

Something must have broken in Gregory's brain, because his focus continuously shifted between the ledger and the bear and the two detectives. Long gone was the cocky, self-confident man from a few minutes ago. "I told you I didn't kill anyone. I couldn't."

Collins's eyes narrowed. "Where were you Saturday night?"

Gregory relaxed and met Collins's accusatory stare. "Is that when it happened? Then I can prove I didn't do it. I was in the ER with my girlfriend's little girl. She had a fever when I got home that afternoon, and we rushed her to the hospital."

Oh my god, this monster was living with another little girl? I flattened my hand on the glass in front of me and wished I could communicate my horror to Flores.

Flores half-faced the two-way mirror as if he could sense me. "Until we can verify your alibi." He pulled handcuffs from the back of his belt, and lifted Gregory up from his chair. The detective turned him around and restrained his hands behind his back in one practiced movement.

"Mr. Willis, you're under arrest for the murder of Albert Johnson." Flores pushed the man to an officer just outside the door. "Book him please."

Collins's face twisted in confusion as soon as the interrogation door closed. "What are you doing? He was talking freely without his lawyer. Now we'll be lucky to get a few grunts."

Flores held up the teddy bear. "I got a tip that Willis abused a little girl, but the caller didn't catch a name. I need to hold him on these charges while I see if I can dig up the victim."

Collins rubbed the top of his bald head. "Man, you youngins are going to wear me to the grave. I'll check out his alibi." Flores's pleading look made the older man sigh. "And I'll take my time."

"Thank you." Flores winked at me through the mirror.

I could breathe again, but we were still no closer to the killer. I left the room to meet Flores and discuss how I could help with the Willis case. I couldn't let him have such intimate contact with a little girl when I knew he'd molested another one. He had to be stopped. The Collector failed to protect those children.

I wouldn't.

Chapter Twenty-Seven

S aturday morning, I opened up Chipped half an hour early. To my delight, Jeff wasn't rolling out of bed, and no remnants of an evening meal littered the floor. A bit of peace and quiet was exactly what I needed. Ironically, it was more peaceful at my place of business, surrounded by non-remnant holding electronics, than at home where Walter's conglomeration of impressions tainted the very atmosphere.

Just as I finished counting the cash drawer and checking the voicemail, the chime on the door rang. I hunkered behind the counter to retrieve Heather's phone, assuming she'd come in to collect it, when my lady bits sensed lust in the air. She must be incredibly grateful her phone was fixed.

I popped up to greet my customer. "She looks good as..." My mouth stopped working as the god-like image of Tucker Wickman stood before me. All those TV medical dramas with their sexy doctors didn't hold a candle to this hunk.

His light blond hair fell across his forehead, as he rubbed the back of his neck. The strong lustful feelings faded to the background and my head started to itch so insistently that I had to squeeze the edge of the counter to stop me from scratching it. What was he anxious about? I didn't surprise him at his work?

I swallowed and put on my customer service face, though I couldn't seem to stop my cheeks from burning. "Hey, Tucker." This wouldn't be the first time a one-night stand tracked me down, but usually we ran into each other at the same club. This was why I didn't take home guys who knew anything about me. Why did I break my rule with Tucker?

"Hey, Fauna." When his eyes met mine with a pleading, instead of accusatory, look, I breathed in a bit easier. That explained why I sensed anxiety, not anger. It was actually kind of adorable; so, I gave him time to get the words out.

"I didn't get your number the other day. And I couldn't remember if I gave you mine." He held up a business card with that medical symbol of the two snakes woven around a winged staff or something like that. On the back, he'd scrawled a phone number. "This is my personal number, you know, if you want to have coffee or dinner or something."

My own indecision froze my mouth. This week had been one so full of change. Was it time to expand my view on relationships? What could it hurt to have coffee with this professional, handsome man who happened to be incredible in bed?

Since I didn't reach out to take the card, Tucker placed it on the countertop. "There's no obligation, mind you. The other night was..." His eyes stared at the piece of cardboard, but my nipples grew extra-sensitive at both his feelings and my own. "I'd like to see you again."

As his eyes met mine, my knees almost buckled. Well shit, I had to break this tension before I took him in the back and sullied Jeff's cot. I pulled my cell phone out and opened my contacts. "A business card? What is this, the 1980s?" After typing in his number, I sent him a smiley-faced emoji. The ding from his pocket told me he received it. "And now you have mine."

My fingers tickled with his happiness as his smile exposed his shiny white teeth. "Good. That's good." He backed up a bit, and I couldn't help but wonder if he also felt the pull to fall into my arms like I did his.

My phone buzzed, breaking the spell. Flores texted.

Flores: *Ron Elstin has reported Debra missing. It might not be related.*

Fear dowsed my playful mood in ice water. "I have to go."

Tucker waved his hands. "I'm sorry. I know I ambushed you at work." He stammered for a minute, but didn't fight as I hurried him to the door. "I'll text you."

His confusion twisted around his after shave. I took pity and placed one gloved hand on his cheek. "You better."

Before he leaned in for a kiss I knew I'd get lost in, I closed and locked the door. I leaned against it for a minute as the thrill of being close to Tucker and the fear of Debra in danger fought within me. There really was no contest. I had to help Debra, and I knew I could. The sadistic killer took his time with George, an actual empath. I could only assume he'd do the same with Debra. As morbid as the thought was, that actually gave Flores time to track him down. Maybe there was a clue that only I could sense at the scene.

I texted Flores.

Me: *I want to help.*

Flores: *Hoped you'd say that.*

After typing the address he gave me into Waze, I tore a shipping box apart to use as a sign. I scribbled, "Family emergency. We're closed. Sorry for the inconvenience," with a sharpie and taped it to the door. What was happening to me? I'd put my heart and soul into this shop. Here I was abandoning it on a Saturday to maybe find a useful impression amongst god knew how many. So maybe I could help a woman I'd just met. I gave my number to a man. I actually hoped he'd call.

If I didn't have to drive all the way to some wealthy neighborhood off Westheimer, I'd stop to get a drink or two first. The overwhelming weight of it all might crush what was left of my sanity if I didn't dull it somehow.

Chapter Twenty-Eight

As I parked behind the now familiar Ford Fusion, the thought of Flores's strong, confident demeanor made me feel safe. I spotted him in the driveway of a two-story home, probably built in the 90s based on its elevation. He spoke with Debra's husband, Ron. I couldn't really think of him as anything but Angry Man. His frantic hand motions and disheveled hair didn't make me reconsider my belief.

When Flores spotted me, he held up a finger to Ron. I couldn't hear him, but whatever he said caused Ron to sit on his front steps and drop his head into his hands.

When the detective got close enough to hear me, I said, "Catch me up."

"Debra never came home from the meeting last night." Flores read notes from his phone while I tried to keep my panic under control. "Ron admits that they had a fight last night. He didn't want her going out, but, as you might guess, she said she had to. He says Debra never slept anywhere but her own bed."

I flicked a tear from my cheek. I understood that well. It was easier to center yourself in places of familiarity. "I can tell if he's lying." Finally, something I could do that could prove helpful.

"How?"

Oh god, this was so hard to explain. "It's more intuition and experience than anything else. There's only one person who's ever fooled me. As on the sleeve of his shirt as Ron is with his emotions, he should be an easy read."

In his signature pose of head down and eyes up, Flores studied me for a second longer than was comfortable. "Let's give it a shot."

The breeze picked up shaking the branches of the bushes in between properties as I followed Flores to Ron. The warm air did nothing to stifle the heat in the late morning air. If the empath killer had Debra, where would he take her? The others were killed in their homes. Maybe it *was* Ron. I didn't know which possibility I preferred. They were both horrific for such a kindhearted woman.

When we got to Ron, Flores perched one foot on the bottom step. "Mr. Elstin, you might remember Ms. Young from the auction Tuesday night?"

While Ron's face flushed red, my stomach clenched with his anger, but it wasn't painful. "The woman who dumped a drink on me? What is she doing here?"

As I removed my gloves and tucked them in my pocket, I thought about my lack of recent practice at this while sober. My curse made it easy to discern whether people were lying or telling the truth. If I truly understood another human being's feelings, I could ask them pointed questions which enabled me to extrapolate. That was how I'd paid for college. I swore when I graduated, I'd never manipulate people for personal gain again. Well, this wasn't for me, right? So, I wasn't breaking any oath.

Before I changed my mind, I reached out my naked hand to Ron. "I'm Fauna Young. I was at the, um, support group meeting with Debra last night. As soon as I heard she never made it home, I wanted to help if I could."

As soon as our hands made contact, a rush of foreign

emotion invaded my sober mind. It was like the most out of control drug you could take. I lost sight of my individuality as Ron's crushing emotions drowned out my own. His fear mixed with guilt and overwhelming worry rolled over anything I felt, it was so intense.

I released Ron and held the stair railing to remain on my feet at the abrupt start and stop of someone else's psyche in my mind.

"He didn't do it," I told Flores. "She really is missing."

Sensing that something happened he didn't authorize, Ron jumped to his feet. "Of course, I didn't do it. Whatever *it* is? Is this some kind of joke to you? She has a heart condition and any stress can send her into arrythmia. We have to find her!"

Flores's voice deepened as he steadied me on the stairs, careful to only touch my clothed, upper arm. "We are taking your concerns seriously, Mr. Elstin. Let me call my partner to get more boots on the ground. If you'll give me a minute, sir." He guided me back toward my car. "Are you sure?"

"I'm sure. He has some guilt, but I'm pretty sure it's from the way he's been acting. His emotions don't have the flavor of lying or hiding anything."

"Flavor?"

Oh shit, I sounded like a crazy person again. "I'm not sure how else to describe it. I'm not used to telling anyone about this process. You'll just have to trust me. You know I want to find her just as much as you do, if not more."

Flores seemed satisfied with my explanation. "Okay. I'll see if Ron has any kind of tracking stuff on his phone."

"Duh, why didn't I think of the technological solution?" I rubbed my forehead to try and dispel the residual effects of the reading. "Let me know if you need help."

The quiet of the neighborhood street offered some peace as my mind cleared. I tried to meditate when I was a teenager. High school was a true nightmare with everyone's emotions and hormones intensified and me having the difficult challenge of separating my own uncontrollable mood swings from everyone else's. I never could quite get the hang of it. My mom thought I got migraines—or at least she called them migraines —and pulled me out of school a lot. If Debra could show me how to succeed where I failed at controlling this ability, maybe I could reenter the regular world without dulling all of my emotions in alcohol before attempting any kind of relationship.

Thoughts of Debra brought up the potential extended trauma on the already bruised empathic group. I believed *they* were alcoholics, when *I* was much closer to one. I couldn't go back and tell them that the killer claimed another of their number. We had to find her.

As I crossed the cracked cement driveway, my shoulder brushed the large boxwood bush between the Elstin's and their neighbor's yard. Anticipation washed through me. What in the hell was that? Bushes don't have emotions.

No more being scared of what I'd see. It was time to act. I stopped and put both hands on the branch.

The world in the memory was dark. Debra stepped out of her car. She was wearing the same clothes from the meeting. The remnant had to have been from a few hours ago.

I couldn't see the person who left the impression since the vision was from his point of view, but I felt anticipation laced with fury, that anger that he kept under his fancy clothes and his manicured nails. It was the empath killer's; I'd recognize it anywhere.

His voice, higher pitched than I would have described it, broke through the silence. "Excuse me, ma'am, have you seen a miniature poodle running around?" He moved toward her, and I lost the impression.

The morning light blinded me when I released the branch. Blinking, I walked up the driveway, looking for Debra's car. I didn't see it.

"Where's her car?" I interrupted Flores's questioning.

Both men turned to me in slow motion. Ron's face deformed into a scowl and Flores's opened in query.

"If I knew that, I wouldn't have called the cops." Ron didn't look happy with the lack of urgency in Flores's apparent inaction.

"Are you sure she didn't stay out last night?" Flores asked.

"She didn't." I walked to the street to take in the parked cars. "One of these must be his or hers."

Flores jogged to keep up with me as I moved down the row. I touched the first car's handle and got nothing.

"What do you mean?"

I pointed to the bush. "He was here. The killer. He left an impression that showed him addressing Debra as she opened the door of *her* car. She did make it home last night, just not in her door." The next car had no impression. Hell, I didn't even know if cars *held* impressions.

With a smooth slide in front of me, Flores blocked me from going any further. "Talk."

"While we were distracted by douchebag child molester, the empath killer must have followed her from the meeting. If Debra's car isn't here, then he took her in it." With a sweep of my arms, I indicated the car-lined street. "Which means—"

"That one of these cars is probably his." Flores dialed a number on his phone. "I'll have Collins compare these plates to the ones at the meeting. He's going to be really happy that I'm bothering him when it hasn't been twenty-four hours yet." He smiled for the first time since I'd met him. His face crinkled as he stared at his screen. "Huh, I missed a call."

With his phone to his face, Flores said, "Collins, I need the list of—" Flores's face flushed and he turned away from me, walking back to his car. He mumbled under his breath.

Annoyed that I couldn't hear him, I jogged to catch up, and cut him off like he'd done me. His face showed no emotion, but he couldn't hide from me. My bare hand gripped his wrist.

My body dragged as the heaviness of grief weighed me down. "No."

I sat on the curb hard, the pain to my pelvis a welcome sensation while the rest of my body grew numb. "We're too late."

After hanging up the phone, Flores joined me on the curb. "I have to tell her husband. But I'm getting you a ride home. You don't need to go to this scene."

For once, I didn't argue. I failed. I couldn't save anyone.

Chapter Twenty-Nine

The emotional impressions from Walter washed over me as I slammed my door shut.

I couldn't believe Debra was gone. I had just met her. I discovered the Collector, another with the same gift who told me to find him, but he was murdered. I found a group of empaths who welcomed me into their fold with Debra as the matriarch. A few hours later, she was sacrificed to this vicious killer who found true joy in tormenting his victims.

The mutilated body of Amethyst invaded my mind, but her terrified face was replaced with Debra's. The anger dripping from that house, from a frustrated psychopath, mixed with the memory's swirling around my apartment.

Curse. I was right the whole time. This stupid ability was a *curse*.

"Dammit!" I yelled. "Leave me alone. What do you want from me?"

Wine was my preferred lubricant at home. This time, I needed something quicker. I reached into the cabinet over the stove for the bourbon. Without bothering with a glass, I took a sip right from the bottle. The part-honey part-fire elixir burned all the way down.

At that moment, I knew I had to get rid of that automaton Walter. I might have been alone before, but my life was peaceful and predictable until that stupid statue came into my life. I grabbed the base and tried to lift it.

My mind ducked into ice water as my body temperature dropped. Splinters drove into my hands as I gripped the pier, but I couldn't see a thing in the dark. I was going to drown.

I ripped my hands from the base. "Fuck you, Collector. You're just as evil as the man who took you. You were supposed to protect those people. Instead you led a murderer to their door."

The beast of a thing wasn't going to win that easily. Another deep drag of bourbon didn't make me any stronger, but it would numb the emotional attacks. I kicked the impression-laden monstrosity. It slammed to my hardwood floor and gouged the shiny surface. I didn't care. It had to go. Nothing else mattered.

The waves in the air tried to speak to me, but I ignored them. Those people were dead, or moved on, or were beyond help one way or another. Why did I need to be tormented by all of their old experiences?

Beyond one piece of an ear, the statue was still in perfect condition. My floor was damaged worse than the ugly thing.

More bourbon numbed the waves no one else could see, as I worked through the problem. "I need a bigger tool."

The kitchen seemed the most logical place to find a weapon. I scoured my drawers for something more damaging than gravity. The best I could come up with was a metal meat tenderizer.

After one more heavy sip, I confronted the offending statue. "I've got you this time. I have no idea if an impression will survive if I destroy it. Let's find out."

No sex, no drink, no night with my girls compared to the satisfaction of bashing the globe head. The piece that was supposed to be my salvation became my affliction. My hands vibrated with the repeated impact of metal on wood. I'd only used the kitchen gadget once or twice. The violence with which chips of people's past flew about my ears was tame compared to the murders I'd witnessed this week.

Either mutilating the piece quieted the combined strength of the signals or the bourbon was working to numb my empathy. One way or another, the room quieted but my arm didn't slow, even as my shoulder started to ache. I gripped the handle with both hands as sweat made my hold slippery. An arm fell off, then the music box twanged as its mechanism was crushed. One ferocious blow broke the head of the tenderizer from the handle. The jagged surface flew at me, though I managed to hit the ground just under its arc.

My elbow grazed a piece of metal bent out from the mutilated body of Walter. Pain blossomed from the cut. It felt refreshing, a bit of my own pain for a change. The statue, however, was not falling apart quickly enough for me.

By half-rolling, half-shoving the piece, I managed to maneuver it to the front door. I wanted it to scream and protest and then grow silent. The noise of all the voices was just too much. I needed Walter to die.

While holding my bleeding elbow with my other hand, I opened my front door and kicked the cursed thing down the outside set of stairs. Wood shards and random tinking sounds filled the air as the concrete finished tearing the offending statue apart. The remnants of what was a human-like automaton smashed into the gate at the bottom of the entrance steps and collapsed into a pile of rubble.

The shards of ex-statue threatened to trip me in revenge as I took one step at a time to witness the results of my violence. I imagined blood instead of debris spreading out from the point of impact like the Collector sprawled on his kitchen floor. The air still vibrated with impressions, but they were muddled, more whispering than a clamoring. Being united like that must have amplified their signal.

My ire and frustration somehow drained, I crouched by the crushed art. His once carefully assembled body lay in divided pieces again, much like the carved and mutilated corpse of Amethyst.

My vision clouded as the horror of the last couple days transformed into heartache. With the handle of the tenderizer still in my grasp, I released my elbow and sorted through the debris. The knife that was the nose on the globe head clunked to the ground. Attached to the handle was a tag with a number on it.

It must have been tucked into the globe all along. All I remembered was a violent murder of a young girl. That's why I hadn't dared touch it again. Now there was a connection. Knowing Albert had tagged certain pieces to use as blackmail, why would he place a valuable piece inside a random art project and send it off into the world? Maybe he never discovered the offender? Maybe the guy died? Whatever the reason, I was much too sick of trying to figure out Albert's motivations to give a damn about why.

As I moved to push the knife aside with the tenderizer handle, my blood-slicked hand slipped and fell on the knife.

Unprepared as I was, the pain, though not even mine, took my breath away. The man holding the knife drove it into the girl's chest as she instinctively grasped at the weapon. This time I tried to push the terror aside. At this point, the bourbon numbing my sensing was a blessing. It helped me separate the experience as not mine.

My instincts screamed at me to just let go, but something about this remnant ticked in the back of my mind. Something I should recognize.

Splattered with his victim's blood, the killer leaned close to the girl's face, a grimace marred his chiseled features, and his eyes glowed the most stunning shade of blue.

Holy shit. Was this the empath killer? The only true emotion I felt was the victim's, likely left from her grasping the knife. With any fear drowned in bourbon, I explored deeper into the remnant. Something else floated behind the girl's terror and panic. It took me a minute to identify, but when I did, I knew for certain this was the same man I searched for. The emotion was joy. I'd never forget that signature.

His deep voice sounded distant through the girl's fading strength. "No one threatens me."

Unwilling to let go until I witnessed everything I could, anything to help me identify this man. I memorized his sleek jawline, his high cheek bones, the way his lip curled up slightly on the left side. I was sure I could describe him to a sketch artist now, but I held on to the end just in case there was more. The girl's gaze drifted to her hands around the knife handle, just above his perfectly manicured nails. A masculine silver ring with a large ruby in the center flashed in the fluorescent light. His shirt sleeves were shredded, and long gashes streaked red on his arms. This was where he got those scars.

Before the scene repeated itself, I dropped the knife. With a deep breath, I took a moment to compose his image in my head. The bourbon made it difficult, but I'd be damned if I was going to lose it now. I tucked my arms around my head, and squeezed my eyes shut, drowning out the neighbor's mewling cat and the searing sun overhead.

His blue eyes floated before me, disembodied. Stop it, brain. I knew more of what he looked like now. A tall, handsome man with the same high cheekbones streaked through my memory. He wore an expensive suit with no tie. I could see him putting on designer sunglasses with long fingers and a *ruby ring*.

It all came back to me in a tsunami of images. I saw that man at the precinct Monday morning. I gagged as I remembered how attracted to him I was. His sunglasses had covered up his eyes. I never even suspected I'd already seen the killer.

My numb fingers reached for my phone in my back pocket. I snapped a picture of the knife with the tag numbers showing and sent it to Flores. Then I dialed his number.

I jumped to my feet, shaking. This was going to be over. This monster would never do this to another empath. "Damn voice-mail. I found another remnant from a murder and it's him, the same guy that killed Albert. We've got him. He was at the precinct Monday morning and the gallery Tuesday night. Get me that sketch artist one more time."

Pain throbbed through my injured elbow as someone grabbed me. Anticipation mixed with anger overrode any of my own emotions. My phone slipped through my fingers as the man dragged me into the alley between my building and the next. He slammed me against the brick wall. I welcomed the pain over the sick feelings of this man invading my soul.

"Get off me." I kicked up, hitting his thigh, instead of my main target.

He released my elbow but held me against the wall with his body weight. His eyes practically glowed blue in the filtered light of the alleyway.

My muscles liquefied as abject horror shook me to my core. The empath killer had me.

He practically licked his lips as he said, "I knew you were one. I saw your face when I touched you."

The voice that had haunted my thoughts since I'd first heard it on the Collector's kitchen floor reverberated in my actual ears. This wasn't an impression or someone else's memory. He was physically here and he knew what I was.

And he was hungry for more.

That realization reignited my flight instinct. I pushed him back with a force born of panic. In a way, he'd killed me four times already. Once through Albert. Once through George. Once through Amethyst. And, finally, through the unknown girl from the knife remnant. He wasn't going to get another chance.

He was so much stronger than me, though. He grabbed both sides of my head and rammed me into the jagged brick. My thoughts jumbled, and I couldn't remember what I'd been trying to do. He bashed my head again, harder, and the world around me faded.

Chapter Thirty

When I blinked myself back to consciousness, my first thought was relief that I was alive. A white ceiling I didn't recognize came into focus. I tried to roll over, but my arms and legs were caught on something. I pulled and tried to sit up, but couldn't. Rope dug into my wrists and my ankles as I struggled to free myself. My eyes watered and my stomach lurched at the fetid smell of unwashed sheets.

My heart jumped as the blue-eyed killer sat down on the side of the bed. Adrenaline fired through my muscles, and I struggled to free myself.

He must have been confident with his knot tying, because he made no move to stop me. With a flip of his wrist, he opened my wallet. "Fauna Young. Such a unique name. My parents had no imagination."

As he reached across my body to shake my opposite hand, I pushed myself as far into the mattress as I could.

"I'm Phil Tanner. We should get to know each other since you'll be here for a while."

My stomach clenched with his deep seeded anger. Missing was the joy floating on top. This was the guy. Why was his signature different in person than on the impressions?

"What do you mean for a while? What do you want with me?" I knew what he wanted with me, but I didn't know why. If I was going to die right after I found my tribe, then I wanted to know *why*.

He ran a finger down my side and along my thigh. This time I felt his anticipation. There was no sexual component in his other attacks, but I got a definite lust vibe from him. What the fuck was going on?

"You know, before that scumbag of an artist, I had never felt joy. Not once in my entire life." He dumped my wallet in a metal trash can and picked up something from the floor. The sharp stench of lighter fluid wafted from the can before a bright orange flash flared from the top.

I stared at the flames of my incinerated identity. He was erasing me. I had to get out of here. Gathering what little I knew about him, I decided to start at the beginning. "Not even when you murdered your lover?" I took an educated guess and hoped for the best.

Phil's eyes focused on me. "How did you know? Did the Collector tell you? That asshole was blackmailing me for that murder. But Sarah asked for it. She threatened to tell my wife and I couldn't have that, now could I."

Holy shit, this madman was married. I prayed to god he didn't have any children.

"But to answer your question, I did find joy in Sarah's demise. There is a certain level of satisfaction that comes from complete and utter control of a person until the very moment of death. Though, at the time, I didn't know that was what I was feeling."

He paced to the other side of the room to peer out of the dingy blinds of a modest window. As he moved, he kicked aside bits of trash and decay piled up along the walls. It looked like a drug den without all of the nasty mattresses piled on the floors.

A bit of light reflected off a set of knives on a side table by the window. George's dissected body flashed into my mind.

"Help!" I screamed with all the energy I could muster.

Phil crossed his arms over his chest and laughed. As if to prove his point, there was no joy in the sound, only knowledge that he knew what I didn't.

"You can scream all you want. No one will hear you. This place has been condemned and the police all but ignore it. I don't know why I didn't think to use it earlier." He picked up an amber-colored bottle and some cotton swaps. "I had it all set up for the psychiatrist. She would have entertained me for days. Sadly, before I got a single cut into her unblemished skin, she simply died."

"Her heart. Her husband said she could die if she was stressed." My heart hurt from beating so hard. I tried to distract him from what seemed inevitable to me now.

"Ah, well that explains it. I assume you're much healthier, aren't you?"

"If I say I'm not, would that make a difference?"

Phil pulled up my shirt. "No. No, I suppose it wouldn't." He dabbed the cotton swab with liquid from the bottle across my stomach.

The cold of the brownish fluid sent goose bumps through my skin. "Iodine? What are you—"

"You see, I've learned a few things and was eager to test them on that woman. We would have had a wonderful time together. Such a waste."

As soon as Phil turned his back, I twisted my right hand back and forth in the tight rope. Maybe I could loosen it.

"I'd stuck around to see if the husband was equally gifted, but that annoying cop showed up before I could make a move. How lucky was I to see you leave Debra's with your gloves? I knew you had to be one." He dipped the knife in a clear liquid that smelled strongly of alcohol, then flashed the surface over a lighter.

He moved toward the bed, the knife still glowed slightly from the flame. "A sterilized blade and a clean surface area keep infection down so we can play longer."

"No, no, no." Nothing else in the world existed beyond the blade as it approached my brown-stained stomach. My body squirmed unable to hold still, no matter how pointless the action was. My instincts screamed to get away.

The point pierced my skin. A sharp pain spread out from the wound just ahead of the oozing blood. I bit my lip and closed my eyes as the pain intensified. Though I didn't look, I could feel the knife slicing through my skin in a shallow cut. The nerves of my abdomen all fired at once.

"Shit," I yelled as loud as I could. "Why are you doing this?"

Phil's eyes shown with madness. "Let me show you."

He flattened a hand just above the draining wound.

My fingertips tingled with joy that washed over the pain, floating on top like an oil slick. Just like I couldn't help yelling from the pain, I couldn't stop myself from laughing. My mind was on fire with the dichotomy of the two opposite emotions.

Phil's deeper laugh joined mine like we were at some sort of seriously sick comedy club. "That's why."

He let me go to pull up a chair by the bed. The burning pain on my stomach flashed back with a vengeance, almost like he'd cut me again.

"Goddammit." My body tried to curl into a fetal position until the bindings did their job. My helplessness burst in the form of tears.

Perched in his chair like a vulture waiting for his dinner to draw its last breath, Phil smeared blood across the brown, turning my stomach into a weird purplish hue. I wouldn't be able to look at that color the same way again.

Even with just the tip of his finger brushing my skin, I felt his happiness at my pain.

"What the hell is wrong with you?" I asked.

He cocked his head at me like it was the dumbest question anyone had ever asked. "We Americans are supposed to pursue happiness. I followed all the rules. I married the prom queen, and felt nothing. I built a real estate empire and became the fifth wealthiest man in Houston. Not a single genuine smile."

He wiped his fingers on a white towel.

"When the legal things didn't work, I tried all the other things. Alcohol, cocaine, mistresses. Not a single hit or single conquest did a thing to move my happiness meter."

I giggled again as he rubbed iodine on the top of my foot. Despite my horror at everything he confessed and the realization that he was about to carve up my foot, I couldn't stop the absorption of his joy. The sick bastard really did feel happy as he caused me pain.

I wanted to say something pithy to distract him or get him to change the topic, but between the pain and the fear and the glee, I couldn't form any words. Too bad I hadn't drained that bottle of bourbon.

"Until one of those mistresses betrayed me. She was going to tell my wife. Some little whore, with no value in this world, thought she could take power from me." He flashed the blade with the lighter again. This time I smelled copper as my blood burned with the alcohol.

"I killed her in a rage. I sat at the kitchen table for an hour, watching her bleed out and I felt something new, something novel, but I didn't know what it was." Phil brought his gaze up to mine. Sharks looked like fuzzy bunny rabbits compared to the cold calculation in this psychopath's eyes.

Then a twinkle hit the corner, and the left side of his mouth angled up. "Let's try something new."

He grabbed my ankle with one hand. Calm washed through me, like a coffee palate cleanser before sniffing more candles. As the knife blade approached the top of my foot, adrenaline fueled panic chased away the calm. This time as he sliced through me, I felt the unrelenting metal against my peeling skin. My breathing intensified in quick bursts which only aggravated the gash in my stomach.

Yet, mingled within the torture was a sense of enjoyment,

pure glee at his power over me. I sucked in a painful breath, then exhaled a laugh. And then did it again. Everything was so intense that I couldn't tell where my emotions began and Phil's ended.

Then Phil let go and laughed with genuine joy.

All confusion fled as every nerve in my body screamed. I could feel the still oozing cut on my stomach, the freely flowing new wound on my foot, the ropes squeezing my ankles and wrists, the pea under the damn mattress. My mind couldn't separate one complaint from another and made them all urgent.

"You see, the Collector tried to blackmail me for what happened to that woman." He twirled the small knife in his hand, and I half expected him to lick the blood off. "Of course, I couldn't allow it. Somehow, he read my emotions and laughed. That's when I knew that weird thing I was feeling was happiness. I finally found happiness. And all I needed were people like you to show it to me."

I had to do something. Helpless was not a state I could tolerate. "Detective Flores is going to find you. You should just let me go now and run for it."

"Won't happen. I'm very good at hiding, but just in case you think about running..." Without his prior dramatic anticipation, Phil jammed the knife into my foot.

My adrenaline had run out leaving me with no buffer to the agony that flared and traveled up my leg. It felt like he'd severed the limb, as the warmth of my own blood gushed under my calf. He twisted the knife and my mind flashed white, then black.

Chapter Thirty-One

When I regained consciousness, it was dark; so I couldn't tell how long I'd been out. My stomach was sore, but somehow tight. I looked down to see a suture Band-Aid closing the clotted wound. He hadn't tended to any of his other victims. He really did want to take his time. How could I tolerate another torture session, let alone many?

I had to get out of here. If I could even walk on my brick of a foot.

The limb he stabbed was completely numb. I was afraid if I attempted to move it, the agony would return and I needed a clear head. The foot was wrapped in layers of gauze, maybe too tightly, which is why it was numb. Blood had soaked through some of the layers, for the top one looked pinkish brown.

More surprisingly, my legs were no longer tied to the end of the bed. I guess Phil figured I wasn't mobile enough to offer a threat of escape. Unfortunately, my hands were still fastened to the headboard. I worked on those ropes, but they held tight.

I did, however, spot a cell phone sitting on the side table. As I stretched my fingers toward my hope of rescue, my foot shifted, and an involuntary gasp escaped my lips at the pain.

"You're awake." Phil's voice sounded chipper. It was creepy, especially when I didn't know he was in the room. How did I not sense him?

"You bound my wounds." It was the only thing I could think of to say. I wanted to get that cell phone, but couldn't see how if my hands were still tied.

His body loomed before me, blocking the yellow light from the lamp in the corner. I couldn't see his face. That was how he must have shadowed himself from his victims where I couldn't get a good look at him. I could feel an undertone of anger surrounding him. At first, I was grateful that my empathic abilities still worked. I didn't want to be treated like poor Amethyst. Then I thought of the anger emanating from the very air in her house.

I didn't want him angry at all if I could help it.

Yet, opening and closing my mouth was all I could manage. Thirst became the next biggest demand of my body over the nerves shouting at me that I was injured. "Can I have some water?"

Phil turned away. At first, I thought he was going for the table with the knives, but he stopped at a small fridge I hadn't noticed earlier.

I used the distraction to reach for the phone again. If I could only tuck it under the pillow, maybe he'd forget about it and I'd have a chance at calling 911. I jumped at the snap of a plastic water cap.

"It won't help you."

I turned on my side and immediately regretted it as my foot shouted its protest. Phil smirked at me with his "I'm smarter than you" look.

Gritting my teeth through the pain, I asked as if I didn't know what he was talking about. "What won't work?"

"The phone." He held the back of my head like a nurse aiding a patient as he poured water gently into my mouth and waited for me to swallow before releasing me. Though I loathed his touch, I welcomed the relief of my parched mouth. "There's no service on it. I just use it for photos."

I was glad my mouth was busy drinking so I couldn't give myself away with a smile. Cell phones were programmed to put through 911 calls with or without service. Then the whole horror hit me. "Wait. You were taking pictures of me?"

"I have to plan ahead. How many like you can there be?" He wiped a bit of spittle from the side of my mouth. He was back to his cold base, and I felt no emotion from him at all. "I never understood the trophies that many of my ilk claim, until I found my joy. I can relive that spark of happiness in the photos on that phone."

"Can I see them?" I had no desire to see them, but I needed to get that phone in my hands.

He rubbed his nose, seeming to consider my request. He reached across the bed and squeezed my bandaged foot.

What had been a minor throbbing flared into a fierce burning. I yanked it away and screamed. "Why?"

Phil grabbed a chef's knife from his table of torture devices. Fear coursed through me and my mind scrambled to come up with a way to avoid the larger blade.

Before I made a decision, Phil leaned over me and cut my hands free. "I had to make sure you couldn't run away."

The rope still clung to my wrists, making them feel swollen. He typed a code into his phone and handed it to me. Propped on the chair between the bed and the door, he watched me with his head cocked as if he were a doctor studying his patient.

My fingers were numb so I couldn't quite get them to obey. What could I do to distract him so I could call 911? As I tried to formulate a plan, I scrolled through the pics. The cut on my stomach throbbed as I saw it in picture form. A tear dropped down from my cheek as the full extent of my injured foot popped onto the screen. The bandage on my real foot covered a grotesque injury.

Most guys begged for boob shots or full frontals. Phil wanted torn skin and oozing wounds. I didn't want to know what he did with these images when he was on his own. He grabbed my ankle, and I flinched. His anger simmered close to the surface, but that tainted joy came along for the ride.

"Some of us have work tomorrow." He spoke like I was wasting his time. "Let's get our full session in before I have to leave."

It was Sunday already? How long had I been out? "No, please. I think my abilities are drained. It won't work right now anyway." I couldn't pretend to be tough. I was just too tired, and I had to pee.

The nostrils of his perfectly shaped nose flared as he brandished the knife in one hand while still gripping my ankle with the other. A wave of anger thrashed through my exhaustion.

It must have shown in my face, because Phil released me with a satisfied grunt. "I think it's working just fine."

I used that bit of anger from him to fuel my inner badass. "Wait. Before we commence the torture of the empath, can I at least use the restroom?"

He squinted at me as if he tried to read my mind.

Even I didn't have that power, asshole.

Then, one corner of his lip rose into the smirk I was starting to hate. Without saying a word, he opened a door fifteen feet from the bed and bowed twirling the knife like a handkerchief inviting a lady to dance. Through the opening, I saw a stained toilet with no lid. Gross. Though not as gross as mixing my urine with my blood already on the mattress.

As I swung my legs to the side of the bed, my injured foot felt like it weighed a thousand pounds. Now I knew why he looked so happy. The anticipation of the pain I'd cause myself as I made it to the bathroom already upped his pleasure quotient.

I squeezed the phone still in my hand as I balanced on my good foot. This damn thing was my only hope. I had to deal with the pain long enough to get to the bathroom and dial 911. With tentative pressure on the toes of my bandage foot, I hopped with the good one. The jarring motion sent agony through the foot that felt larger than the space it actually took up.

Phil laughed and leaned against the door jamb, crossing his ankles and arms. Maybe this pain would fulfill whatever sick need he had, and he wouldn't carve more holes in my body today.

I hop-skipped my way to the bathroom threshold before taking a break against the moldy drywall. I felt like I'd just run a marathon in those fifteen feet. I wasn't even sure I had to pee anymore, but I was going to attempt it. Salvation was just a phone call away.

The last foot and a half to the toilet was the hardest of the whole trip. As I pivoted on my good foot while using the back of the toilet as a crutch, I gestured at Phil to close the door.

He shrugged, but complied. "In the end, there will be no need for modesty. Intimate isn't descriptive enough for what we will be."

The shiver that ran through my body had nothing to do with temperature. As soon as the door clicked, I scrolled up on the phone and dialed 911. I muted the speaker and tucked the phone behind the toilet. Hopefully, I could keep him distracted long enough for HPD to find me. The shiny triangle of the chef's knife flashed through my mind. He certainly didn't seem in a hurry to end it.

Turns out I really did need to pee. Without any toilet paper, I tore the bandage from my stomach and used that. A scraping sound from the door made me jump and jam my foot hard on the dingy floor.

"Dammit!" I yelled. "I'm coming. You don't have to make creepy noises to scare me."

Phil flung the door open as I pulled my leggings up, careful to leave them below my belly button. The newly exposed cut burned in the air.

"I can't wait forever. We're on my schedule, not yours." He draped my arm over his shoulder and guided me to the bed much faster than I could have managed on my own. The handle of the knife scraped my side as we walked. I wished I was a martial arts expert and knew how to perform some sort of fancy twist to disarm him. As it were, even if I did know how, I didn't think I could have mustered enough energy to pull it off.

He set me on the bed and swung my legs delicately up. The tenderness was surreal since he intended to carve me like a Thanksgiving turkey.

With a new rope in his hand, he motioned for me to lay back down. I wanted to run, but my pierced foot would only let me stumble. For now, it was best for me to play along until the police found me. I wasn't really the wait in a tower for my prince kind of girl, but I didn't see any other option.

Phil stretched my arms over my head re-opening the cut on my stomach. My body curled up as a gasp escaped my lips.

He straightened me out to examine his handy work. "Where did your bandage go?"

"Typical man seems to have forgotten the toilet paper. I had to improvise."

He cocked his head at the bathroom, then shot his gaze back to me. "Where's the phone?"

Chapter Thirty-Two

My face burned as my exhausted brain tried to come up with something clever. "I gave it back to you."

His forehead crinkled. "No, you didn't," he said, even though he checked his pockets anyway.

He forced my chin up with the tip of the blade. "Don't move."

I whimpered as the tip cut my skin. I couldn't answer without moving my jaw. My vision blurred as I pictured the blade piercing my face like the smaller one had my foot. There wasn't enough adrenaline left in my abused body to mask any of the pain. Tears flowed down the side of my face and pooled at my ears. Maybe I should have fought harder.

My weakness seemed to satisfy him as he relieved the pressure and moved to the bathroom. He would find the phone and see it dialed to 911. He would know I called. I would experience his rage firsthand. Would Flores employ another empath to sense it secondhand?

As my chance of rescue evaporated, I had to escape on my own. But how? What power did I have to get out of his grasp?

Biting my tongue to keep my mouth shut, I flung my feet over the side of the bed and sat up in one swift movement. The pain was minor compared to my level of panic. I had to get out of there.

"What have you done?" His voice echoed from the bathroom, a demon shouting from the depths of hell.

I fell to my knees as my foot refused to hold my weight. Maybe I could scoot to the hallway and barricade the door from the outside? Please, oh please, I had to get away. Part of me decided to attack Phil outright, make him so angry he would kill me quickly, and the pain would end.

My head shot backward as Phil yanked my hair. He had to have flown across the room, because I didn't hear any footsteps.

He stomped on my foot. I screamed and collapsed. The thunk of my head on the floor seemed to happen to someone else, because all I could feel was the agony emanating from my foot. It overrode any other sensation, blocked any other thought.

He flipped me on my back and straddled my stomach. His blue eyes shown in the dim room like spotlights. For a moment, I thought I was experiencing the Collector's last moment again.

My arms flew up to protect my face. Then a sharp pain ripped through my right forearm.

My confused senses couldn't tell where my sensations ended and where Phil's emotions began. Is this what the Collector felt? The first empath to meet this fate, to feed this psychopath his own selfish emotions.

"You've ruined our time together, but don't think you have a bit of power over me." Phil held my uninjured wrist and sliced my forearm in three quick strokes.

I screamed. My emotions swam from agony to joy to anger to desperation. Which ones were mine and which were his? I had avoided touching people my whole life, so I wouldn't have to separate these feelings, so I wouldn't have to empathize.

So, I wouldn't lose myself.

I'll be damned if this cold son of a bitch would be the one to push me over the edge. It was time to take back control. If I was going to die today, it would be with my *own* emotions flowing through my veins, my own psyche in control.

I squirmed as my will kicked back in. Though he was much stronger, I wasn't going down without a fight. His hand on mine radiated anger through my being. I took advantage of it and claimed the fierce emotion as my own.

The rage gave me strength. With his knife wielding hand posed over my chest, I punched him in the stomach with both hands, knocking the wind out of him.

He dropped the knife as his anger morphed to surprise. My blood pooling on the floor made the old tile slippery enough for me to flip on my side underneath him and dive for the weapon.

He crawled on all fours after me and smashed my head into the ground, stunning me. Phil retrieved his knife before I could shake myself back into action. I shifted as he dived at me and the knife sunk into my shoulder. I could feel the pain, but with my exhaustion, it was more like pressure.

The blade must have become to slippery, because on his next upward stroke, it flew out of his hands.

Whatever he cut in my shoulder removed all control of my arm. This couldn't last much longer.

Phil yelled in frustration and scrambled to his feet, heading to the torture instruments table by the window. Before I reached the door to the hallway, his weight fell over me again. I swore he'd gotten heavy. Phil pushed a finger into the torn flesh around the blade wound on my shoulder. My scream was cut off by his happiness at my pain.

I laughed over my sobs.

"You see, you should have cooperated. You would have lived much longer, and enjoyed it almost as much as me. George Martinez died with a smile on his face."

It wasn't fair. How could he do that? Usurp my feelings, my emotions, and replace them with his own when he claimed to have so little. I could experience Phil's joy and anger, but he couldn't feel my pain.

The closest thing I'd ever seen to a two-way conversation emotionally was the Collector leaving his message on the globe. That had been intentional, not an accident of chance like most impressions. My mind kept going back to the message, the omen that ultimately led to my murder. There was something there, something I could use, if only I could focus long enough to come up with a plan.

My lips parted in laughter. I screamed in my mind at the traitorous bits of my body. The pain was mine. I didn't want to give him more joy by being the living lie detector that translated his own emotions for him.

Phil wrenched my wrists over my head—making sure his skin always touched mine—and straddled my body. I kicked my legs but couldn't dislodge him. With quick, practiced strokes, he slashed the meatiest part of my arm.

The pain intensified as I struggled, my very act of resistance opened my wounds wider. A wash of Phil's joy made me laugh.

Phil laughed with me. "I thought I'd won the lottery when I found that meeting of people like you. It was like a whole herd of food for a hungry lion. And you've been the best meal so far. Too bad I have to end it so soon." He ripped apart my shirt and scraped the knife between my breasts, almost tenderly.

My peripheral vision faded as blackness clawed at my conscious mind. My pain dulled. My empathy faltered. In what could be my last moment, I found clarity. Each feeling was played on a different frequency. If I focused on one, I could reproduce it and impress a living memory on an object. I knew it to be true as much as I knew I was bleeding to death.

"You know what?" The words snuck out of my clenched teeth. "I'm done entertaining you."

The empath killer pushed the tip of the thin, boning knife into the skin just above my heart. "Oh, are you?"

This time I embraced the pain. I focused on every nerve and let the agony of each injury swell in my mind. The sensation was so intense I almost passed out again. Instead, I concentrated on its energy signature.

With his other hand, Phil poked at the wound on my shoulder. I screamed but kept my focus on the pain instead of trying to run from it. Phil smiled as he placed his other hand flat over the shoulder wound. His happiness tried to coat my agony, but I blocked it.

His forehead crinkled and his smile dropped. "What's happening?"

I bit my tongue when he twisted the tip of the boning knife on my sternum. The taste of my own blood only strengthened my resolve.

His joy turned to anger. I could feel the change, but I refused to reflect it. It was much easier to block them as soon as I recognized the frequency.

I looked into his crisp blue eyes that shined with joy at his complete power over me. And I knew. It was time for Phil to feel what I did.

I would leave my impression on him.

Instead of the knife handle, I squeezed his wrist with my one working hand. By bundling the pain from my foot and my shoulder and the cuts and puncture wounds on my chest and arms, I forged a ball of agony as a weapon, and forced it through my hand into Phil.

Shock flashed across his face as he cried out and fell to his side. He looked at his foot as if someone had attacked him. Someone had, but he looked in the wrong direction.

I could only take short breaths. All of my strength focused on holding his wrist and funneling my pain into Phil.

I wrapped my good leg around his waist so he couldn't pull away. I didn't know how much longer I could keep holding, but he would feel it *all* before I died. His left arm fell to his side as I shared my agony and helplessness with my attacker.

Phil looked up in horror. "What are you doing?"

This time the happiness was my own. Every time he decided

to slice up another of my kind, he would remember my pain and his joy would be tainted.

My fingers loosened as my vision flashed red. Phil yanked his hand back and rolled my weakened leg off him. He took a deep, relieved breath.

The anger must have radiated from him again as he seemed to have an unending supply, but I could no longer feel anything. My muscles gave up their fight and my body flopped against the peeling linoleum. My vision narrowed and lost focus.

A shadow of the monster lifted the knife high overhead in a double-handed grip. A snarl escaped his lips, but no words.

As the knife came down, I heard a shout from behind me. Phil's head angled up, but the knife continued toward my heart.

Two explosions in quick succession tore open Phil's chest. He dropped the knife and collapsed beside me.

The last thing I saw as the darkness claimed me was his icy blue eyes fade to a dull lifeless hue.

Chapter Thirty-Three

W hen I woke up, my body squeezed against itself like I was still bound to that bed, but this time more securely. Shocked to still be alive, I took in a quick, panicked breath. Pain shot through my torso on the inside and ripped through my skin on the outside. I cried out and tried to focus on my surroundings to access the danger I was in.

"Shh." Detective Flores gripped my hand, gentle warmth relaxed my tense muscles as his calm drained my panic. "You're safe, Fauna. He's gone."

As my logical mind took in the clues, rubbing alcohol floating over sickness, push tile ceilings, crisp, bleached sheets, I relaxed into the mattress, relieved to be in a hospital.

I smiled at him through my tears. "Those explosions I heard were you."

His face darkened. "I had no choice. He didn't drop the knife." He rubbed his nose with his other hand. "I wasn't even sure you were still alive until I found a weak pulse."

"*I* wasn't sure I was still alive." I tried to sit up, but my right shoulder screamed at me. "Shit, everything hurts. I guess that means I'm going to make it."

Flores chuckled. "I'll get the doctor to do something about the pain."

"It's not that bad. Those things make me loopy." I had too many questions to be knocked out with pain meds. "How did you find me?"

"I compared the license plate numbers on the street to the ones Collins recorded from the community center. We got a match for Philip Tanner, real estate mogul. We couldn't get a warrant on such circumstantial evidence. When you and I got disconnected, I found the knife handle with the tag like you mentioned and matched that to an anonymous bank account from offshore in the Collector's ledger.

"We didn't know for sure it was Tanner's, but it was the same kind of set up we'd seen before with wealthy perpetrators. Collins and I split up his properties to look for you. When a 911 call was disconnected at the abandoned property, I was closest. Debra's car was outside one of the buildings, which is where I started to look. When I heard you," he cleared his throat, "scream, I was able to pinpoint your exact location."

"What happened after you shot Phil Tanner?" Saying his name made my bandaged foot itch. Would it always do that?

"He won't hurt anyone ever again."

"Enough of the cryptic. Does that mean he's dead or going to jail? You know these powerful people can get away—"

Flores stood and shoved his hands in his pockets. "He's dead. Two shots was all it took."

Somehow, I felt if Flores still held my hand, I would feel his guilt. "That man would never have stopped. He couldn't."

With his head slightly cocked, Flores said, "But now we'll never know why he did what he did."

"I know exactly why. It was the only sense of joy he ever experienced, torturing others. And he didn't trust his own feelings unless they were reflected through an empath." I stared at the ceiling. "Though no one will ever believe that explanation."

"I do." Flores's support meant more to me than he would

ever know. "Who knows, I might need a consultation sometimes."

"I would be honored." I winked at him. "For a small fee."

Flores laughed, the way someone should laugh, with true happiness, not sadistic glee. God, I prayed I'd be able to get Phil's cackle out of my head.

My hospital door busted open. I jumped, then moaned at the pain along the length of my body. Flores blocked me as best he could with his own body and put his hand on his side arm.

Amelia argued with a nurse who was trying to keep her out. "We *are* her family, and no one is stopping us."

Gina's shiny, dark hair bounced in front of the confrontational nurse and practically pushed Flores aside. She put both hands on my cheeks, making my eye twitch. "Fauna, we were so worried. Your townhouse looked like a war zone, and you weren't answering your phone."

An imposing figure held the door open. Collins's heavy voice assured the nurse. "It's alright, Harriet. Police business."

Amelia said, "Detective Collins stopped by while we were cleaning and told us where to find you." She took Gina's hands off my face, though I really didn't mind her tender touch after all I'd been through.

Gina flung a tear from her eye. "We'll get you out of here as soon as possible." She bent down to whisper, "I can't imagine how emotionally draining this place must be for you."

I assured them. "I'm sure I'll be out of here in no time."

Amelia studied me for a moment. "You're kind of blue."

Gina shook her head and frowned. "Fauna simply hasn't had time to put on her make up yet what with capturing a serial killer and all."

I laughed, then grimaced at the pain in my chest. "Don't make me laugh."

Now Amelia's face flushed red. Maybe I wouldn't go into detail about what happened. Though, knowing the crime drama shows we all watched together, the ins and outs of what happened would have to be shared eventually. At least I didn't have to lie to them anymore.

"You have quite an eclectic family, Ms. Young." Tucker strode into the room in green scrubs and a shiny white coat. It took a second to realize he must work here. I patted my hair, wishing I'd had time to freshen up. "Let's clear out for now while I talk to Ms. Young about her diagnosis and recovery."

Collins ushered my friends to the hallway. "Let's go, ladies. I still need to get your full statements anyway."

Gina kissed me on the forehead. "We'll be right outside."

Amelia nodded her chin in my direction. "As soon as doc's done, we'll be right back in."

The nurse, who had tried to keep them out, harrumphed as the crowd departed. While Tucker stared at Flores, the nurse stood beside my bed with her arms crossed.

With his chin down and eyes up, Flores planted his feet.

His authoritative presence didn't seem to bother Tucker.

I raised an eyebrow at him. "Detective Flores is alright. You can talk freely in front of him."

Tucker's mountain sky blue eyes shown with such tenderness, I couldn't think why I'd suspected him of being a killer for even a second. His fingers drummed on his clipboard. "I was on duty in the ER when they brought you in."

One look between Flores and Tucker made my heart heavy and light at the same time. "I guess I have two heroes then."

Chapter Thirty-Four

The cute, little, blue house with the semi-wraparound porch was hidden behind a humungous live oak tree. The cracked sidewalk offered a new obstacle for my crutches. Most of my wounds had heeled with minimal scaring. Though I'd never wear a tank top again without getting funny looks, and my career as an Olympic runner was over.

Gina walked close to me with her arms braced just in case I stumbled. "Are you sure we shouldn't have brought the wheelchair? Your foot is so much better. I don't want you to fall and reinjure it."

On my other side, Amelia carried a large paper bag full of hard cider and craft beer. She was having just as much trouble as I was. "Leave her be, Gina. She's not one of your second graders."

After I told them about my empathic abilities, our relationship hadn't changed. For that, I would be forever grateful.

Gina admired the old English garden's smoothly painted picket fence. "This does not look like the kind of place barely-talks-at-all Flores would live."

Amelia pushed the gate open and guided me through. I swear she'd carry me if she could. "Well, he doesn't live alone does he."

The red-painted front door opened at the top of the stairs, sending a wind of cold air into the heat of Houston fall.

Flores hopped down the stairs in khaki shorts and a Hawaiian shirt. His beefy chest filled out the loose button up while his short and tight hair screamed military.

Gina coughed into her elbow to hide a girlish giggle.

Amelia leaned in to whisper in my ear. "Does he have a straight brother?"

"You made it." He held his arms out and cocked his head, asking for permission.

"You better give me a hug," I said.

He embraced me firmly without aggravating a single tender spot. I soaked in the warmth of his affection.

"That better be Fauna Young you're hugging and not our cute new neighbor." A stunningly handsome, white man with spiked blond hair and pearly whites crossed his arms on the porch in mock jealousy.

Flores shook his head on my shoulder as he released me. His contentedness flowed through his cheek and gave me hope that happy couples did exist. Tucker and I had seen a lot of each other over the last few weeks, but it was in a more professional sense. I hadn't had the energy, emotional or physical, to pursue anything else. For now, just being alive was enough.

I swung on my crutches to the bottom step. "You must be Austin. It's a pleasure to meet you."

Austin looked delighted that I knew his name. "So, he does talk about me at work."

With a heavy sigh, Flores flung his arm around Austin's shoulders. "I can't help it. You call me every hour or so."

Austin feigned hurt feelings as he brushed Flores off him. Instead, he guided me around the steps to a path on the side of the house. "We have so much to talk about."

The backyard BBQ could have been taken out of a magazine. The crowd was diverse in a way that looked forced in a picture, but felt so natural for this part of Houston. Lanterns hung from the thick branches of old growth trees. A pool too small to be more than a soaking tub bubbled away in a corner. An all-weather TV hung on the back of the house playing a baseball game.

Flores set me down in a chair under a tree. "If you need some air conditioning, let me know and we'll impress a few strong men to help you up the stairs."

I laughed and was happily surprised when it didn't hurt. There was a light at the end of the tunnel.

Gina dropped a cider in my hand. "You realize when you're all healed, it's your turn to wait on me hand and foot."

I gripped the cool drink in my gloved hand. "A task I will relish."

Austin finished with the group he was talking to and joined us.

Amelia raised her eyebrows at the host. "You sure know how to work a party, Austin. I'm not sure how you put up with all business Flores."

Flores lifted his chin. "He needs me to pick up the heavy things."

"And a few other chores." Austin swatted his husband. "Flores enjoyed working with you on this tough case. He told me you had some insight he didn't have access to."

I twirled the crutch on the ground wondering how much Flores had told Austin. "I have a few skills."

Flores stopped the crutch with his foot, forcing me to look up at him. "She's going to consult with HPD when we have a particularly tough case."

His words rang true. What's the point of having this gift if I didn't use it to help others? Sure, it made me the target of a serial killer, but it also helped me stop a child molester and prevent an innocent kid from going to prison. I can't imagine what the line item on the police bill would be, but I could see me working with Flores.

"Of course, if you need any computer work done, I'm your girl."

A general cheer from the guests announced a home run by the Astros on the screen. I added my voice to the chorus.

This was my city. If I could help protect it, I would.

Acknowledgments

A book cannot exist without a plethora of contributors. I've been lucky enough to have a team that helps bring the magic to life. I must thank Ashley Hartsell for her incredible insight as my editor. Without her, the book would be choppy at best. My beta readers bravely dived in to give me their valuable feedback. Thank you to Jessica Raney, Chisto Healy, and Jill Valuet for your generous and critical observations. Kailey Urbaniak did an excellent job catching my inconsistencies and odd sentence structures. Thank you for copy editing and allowing the work to shine. I have to give a very special thank you to Stefanie Saw for the gorgeous cover. She exceeded anything I could have imagined. Finally, I have to thank my husband, Kevin. None of this would exist without his never ending support of my passions and Cursed Dragon Ship Publishing.

About the Author

Kelly Lynn Colby has always been curious about the abilities hidden within the human psyche. In her new series, Emergence, she explores the world through the eyes of people with such gifts. Though this novel is a bit different from her first foray into publishing with *Tarbin's True Heir*, a traditional epic fantasy, Kelly still can't keep magic out of her writing. Kelly writes about the fantastical at her cluttered desk, coffee shops, and parks, mostly in Houston, Texas. You can follow her adventures by joining her newsletter at **https://tinyurl.com/y4qn2crq** or the social media of your choice below.

facebook.com/kcolbywrites

twitter.com/kcolbywrites

instagram.com/kcolbywrites

Also by Kelly Lynn Colby

Also by Kelly Lynn Colby

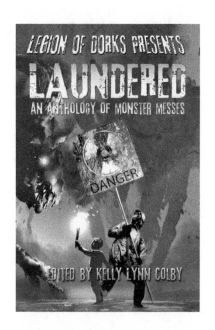

Also by Cursed Dragon Ship

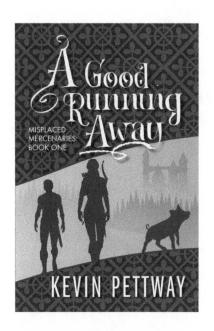

CPSIA information can be obtained
at www.ICGtesting.com
Printed in the USA
BVHW071049280121
598991BV00001B/228